DEFENDER

A Story Of Angels And Demons

Brent Jackson

ISBN 978-1-63961-969-6 (paperback)
ISBN 978-1-63961-970-2 (digital)

Christian Faith Publishing
832 Park Avenue
Meadville, PA 16335
www.christianfaithpublishing.com

Printed in the United States of America

For my wife Wendy,
My best friend, my greatest encourager.
A heart full of kindness that knows no bounds.

*H*e looked horrific; a monstrous madness displayed completely in his malicious face. Lucifer was a beautiful savage, ready to rip apart anything that stood in his way. His blade, the bloodthirsty Abaddon, caught fire. Horns began to emerge from his forehead, and a strange star became visible on his chest. There were symbols in the star. A black smoke came from both his nostrils and ears. He smelled of death. In his left hand, he held a ball of fire. The prophecy was going to be destroyed... Only the angels of heaven stood in his way...

PROLOGUE

1 Samuel 25

David moved down into the desert of Maon. A certain man in Maon, who had property there at Carmel, was very wealthy. He had a thousand goats and three thousand sheep, which he was shearing in Carmel. His name was Nabal, and his wife's name was Abigail. She was an intelligent and beautiful woman, but her husband, Nabal, was surly and mean in his dealings.

While David was in the desert, he heard that Nabal was shearing sheep. So he sent ten young men and said to them, "Go up to Nabal at Carmel and greet him in my name. Say to him: 'Long life to you! Good health to you and your household! And good health to all that is yours!' Now I hear that it is sheep-shearing time. When your shepherds were with us, we did not mistreat them, and the whole time they were at Carmel, nothing of theirs was missing. Ask your own servants, and they will tell you. Therefore, be favorable toward my young men, since we come at a festive time. Please give your servants and your son David whatever you can find for them."

When David's men arrived, they gave Nabal this message in David's name. Then they waited.

Nabal answered David's servants, "Who is this David? Who is this son of Jesse? Many servants are breaking away from their masters these days. Why should I take my bread and water, and the meat I have slaughtered for my shearers, and give it to men coming from who knows where?"

David's men turned around and went back. When they arrived, they reported every word. David said to his men, "Put on your swords!" So they put on their swords, and David put on his. About four hundred men went up with David, while two hundred stayed with the supplies.

One of the servants told Nabal's wife Abigail, "David sent messengers from the desert to give our master his greetings, but he hurled insults at them. Yet, these men were very good to us. They did not mistreat us, and the whole time we were out in the fields near them, nothing was missing. Night and day, they were a wall around us all the time we were herding our sheep near them. Now think it over and see what you can do because disaster is hanging over our master and his whole household. He is such a wicked man that no one can talk to him."

Abigail lost no time. She took two hundred loaves of bread, two skins of wine, five dressed sheep, five seahs of roasted grain, a hundred cakes of raisins, and two hundred cakes of pressed figs and loaded them on donkeys. Then she told her servants, "Go on ahead, I'll follow you." But she did not tell her husband Nabal.

As she came riding her donkey into a mountain ravine, there were David and his men descending toward her, and she met them. David had just said, "It's been useless, all my watching over this man's property in the desert so that nothing of his was missing. He has paid me back evil for good. May God deal with me, be it ever so severely, if by morning I leave alive one male of all who belong to him!"

When Abigail saw David, she quickly got off her donkey and bowed down before David with her face to the ground. She fell at his feet and said, "My lord, let the blame be on me alone. Please let your servant speak to you. Hear what your servant has to say. May my lord pay no attention to that wicked man Nabal. He is just like his name, his name is fool, and folly goes with him. But as for me, your servant, I did not see the men you sent... Please forgive your servant's offense, for the Lord will certainly make a lasting dynasty for you, my master, because you fight the Lord's battles. Let no wrongdoing be found in you as long as you live. Even though someone is pursuing you to take your life, the life of my master, David, will be bound securely in the bundle of the living by the Lord your God. But the lives of your enemies, he will hurl away as from the pocket of a sling. When the Lord has done for my master every good thing he promised concerning him and has appointed him leader over Israel, my master will not have on his conscience the staggering burden of needless bloodshed or of having avenged himself. And when the Lord has brought my master success, remember your servant."

David said to Abigail, "Praise be to the Lord, the God of Israel, who has sent you today to meet me. May you be blessed for your good judgement and for keeping me from bloodshed this day and from avenging myself with my own hands. Otherwise, as surely as the Lord, the God of Israel, lives, who has kept me from harming you if you had not come quickly to meet me, not one male belonging to Nabal would have been left alive by daybreak."

Then David accepted from her hand what she had brought him and said, "Go home in peace. I have heard your words and granted your request."

When Abigail went to Nabal, he was in the house holding a banquet like that of a king. He was in high spirits and very drunk. So she told him nothing until daybreak. Then in the morning, when Nabal was sober, his wife told him all these things, and his heart failed him, and he became like a stone. About ten days later, the Lord struck Nabal, and he died.

When David heard that Nabal was dead, he said, "Praise be to the Lord, who has upheld my cause against Nabal for treating me with contempt. He has kept his servant from doing wrong and has brought Nabal's wrongdoing down on his own head."

Then David sent word to Abigail, asking her to become his wife. His servants went to Carmel and said to Abigail, "David has sent us to you to take you to become his wife."

Abigail got on a donkey and, attended by her five maids, went with David's messengers and became his wife.

David and Abigail had a son named Daniel, whom she liked to call Chileab, because he was so much like his father.

CHAPTER 1

White was everywhere. The sky was white, the trees were white, the ground was white, but not a blinding white. The white was a pure white, of which no blemish could be detected. It was perfect, and it was pure, and it was peaceful. Only the crystal blue water that flowed through the valley was distinguishable from the white. The water was clear and fresh and crystal, having no beginning and no ending. It was neither hot nor cold in the valley, neither dark nor bright; the air was perfectly still as there was no movement. The river flowed south to north, with enormous trees on the east and west banks. Thousands upon thousands of trees, all white, all strong, all tall, with limbs upon limbs expanding out of the tops. There seemed to be a hierarchy among the trees, with the tallest and strongest located far north. As trees moved southward, the height and prestige of the trees seemed to descend as well. The northeastern bank of the valley was home to the tree of trees, the tallest and strongest and most magnificent. Life was in the trees. Each treetop was filled with eyes staring out upon the valley. The eyes were golden and seemed to be hidden within the whiteness of the trees. Eyes that were still, did not blink, and seemingly could see everything.

A wall surrounded the valley, a wall that seemed to be constructed out of white crystal with an indescribable strength and pureness emanating from it. The wall appeared to have its own energy as it spread around the valley. The height of the wall was unknowable as it reached skyward, perfectly meshing with the whiteness of the sky.

The energy of the wall would allow it to reach to the end of the sky, and there was no weakness or vulnerability anywhere as the impregnable energy breathed into the valley. The wall met with a huge gate at the southern end of the crystal waters of the river. The gate was the only way into or out of the valley. The gate was controlled by the same energy source as the wall and could reach to the heights of infinity. The gate had been constructed out of a combination of gold and bronze, and any living being would find it impossible to come within ten feet of the gate without having the permission of the gatekeeper. The gatekeeper existed within the gate and answered to only one.

A field was located at the northern end of the valley. A field of complete whiteness situated perfectly to the east of the river directly in front of the tree of trees. The dimensions were impossible to ascertain as the field could seemingly expand and contract as needed. The field was the place for activities such as meetings, praise, training. The stillness in the valley seemed as if it could go on forever or could end at any moment. There was no concept of time, no concept of day and night, no worry, no anxiety, no feeling of beginning or ending. Peace seemed to permeate the air, and strength was felt all throughout the valley, especially in the north. Thousands of golden eyes in thousands of trees, all seemingly waiting for something. This was the Valley of Eternity, the Home of Angels. The gatekeeper was Ishboth, and as if from nowhere, he appeared out of the gate. Ishboth was not big, but a quiet strength permeated his presence. He had no wings, no robes, no sword but rather was equipped with a long strip of leather. As if on command, he threw the strip of leather around the gate and began to pull. The gate opened to the inside, and as it opened, bells sounded throughout the valley, heavenly bells sounding as if they had been created to announce the arrival of a being into the Valley of Eternity. On cue, all trees instantly began to move and heavenly beings, almost as one, standing on air in front of their trees.

They did not bow to the figures entering the gate but rather stood erect as a sign of respect. Respect for the archangel, angel of angels, glory of glories, leader of leaders, for the heavenly beings were watching the entrance of Michael.

Michael sat atop a giant white horse with a long flowing white mane. The eyes of the horse were fire, and a holy mist came out of his mouth, and the name of the horse was Pran. He walked as if he were the king of horses, head held high and proud. On the back of Pran was Michael, an aura of light surrounding him; he was in the form of a man with wings of gold protruding out of his shoulders. He carried a huge sword on a belt of gold wrapped around his waist. There was an air of majesty and leadership from Michael. His face was white, his eyes golden, his long hair flowed behind his back. His face had the features of a man, yet without facial hair and without emotion. On his body was a tunic made of bronze, and on his feet were leather boots that wrapped around his shins almost up to his knees. Michael wore no helmet. The wings were huge and seemed to be made of golden feathers, each feather filled with sparkling glow. Muscles bulged from his arms and his legs, and it was clear that this warrior was the chief angel in the Valley of Eternity. Uniquely situated directly behind Michael was a second horse, this one white also, but not as white as Pran. This horse was slightly off-white and not nearly as large. Following obediently, on the back of the second horse sat another angel, clearly subservient and without the aura and light of Michael. This angel was Uri and was the armorbearer for Michael. He too had wings protruding from his shoulders, though not as large, and he too had muscles surrounding his bronze tunic. Behind Uri was a third horse.

All eyes in the valley went to the third horse, a white-and-black Appaloosa, of which none of the eyes in the valley had ever seen before. This was not a heavenly horse and required both saddle and bit to be controlled. On the back of the Appaloosa sat a figure of a boy, but not just any boy, a human boy. As far as the angels in the valley could remember, no human had ever entered the Valley of Eternity. Appearing to be around the age of twelve, the boy sat atop the saddle and entered through the gate, eyes looking straight ahead, back upright, refusing to stare at any of the amazing sights before him. He had clearly been coached by Michael to sit straight and proud and not gaze too long in any direction, to be respectful of his surroundings and under no circumstance was he to speak without first being spoken to. The boy tried to hold the fear inside of him. He wanted to cry, but he knew, as Uri had told him, he was to remain strong, for there was no weakness to be found among the angels. The three horses slowly made their way to the northern end, stopping in front of the tree of trees and turning to face the valley. Thousands of angels were standing in front of trees, the bells had ceased ringing as Ishboth had closed and secured the gate. Michael and Uri's wings lifted them off their horses, and a small angel with no wings came to take the reins of the Appaloosa as the boy climbed down. Pran and the two other horses were led through the river to the other side and disappeared into the huge trees on the northwestern bank. Michael began to sing in a language the boy had never heard before, and his eyes filled with water. Uri poked him in the back and spoke to him in his language, "Remember, boy, no emotion." Michael continued to sing,

> *Praises be the Lord of Lords.*
> *Praises be our Lord of Lords,*
> *The maker of angels, the maker of men, the maker*
>   *of earth, and the maker of heaven,*
> *He is our God,*
> *He is our God,*
> *He is Lord of All.*

The boy could not understand anything Michael was singing as he sang for what seemed like forever. His mouth was dry, and he felt as if he were about to pass out so the boy turned his head slightly to ask Uri if he could have a drink of water. Uri slapped him hard on the back of the head and replied, "You will stand tall and strong, and say nothing, you will let Michael do the talking." The boy had no idea what Uri meant by "let Michael do the talking" and was about to ask when suddenly Michael grabbed him around the waist, and he was lifted into the air. He could feel the power in Michael and the power in his wings and suddenly had no fear.

High above the tallest of trees in the middle of the Valley, Michael and the boy stopped in midair. The wings continued to move powerfully, yet there was no sound, until Michael's voice boomed out throughout the valley. "Angels of the Valley, Our Lord sends his greetings with a special request of us. His order for me was to enter the dimensions of the earth and locate this boy and bring him to our home. We are to accept him, train him, discipline him, and teach him the ways of the angel. He is to learn our language, our customs, our strength, and our mission. He will be under the eyes of all, yet he will have one specific teacher in charge of his instruction. Our Lord has chosen his instructor, and it shall be Hagan."

Hagan, surprised, stepped out away from his tree and instantly bowed before the valley. Michael continued, "Hagan, you are the angel chosen by our Lord to lead the instruction of the boy. There will be no debate, for this is of the Lord." The eyes of angels throughout the valley focused on Hagan, and more than a few looked briefly at each other. Hagan stood as straight as possible, and his angelic frame was tall and thin. His hair was pulled back behind his head in a ponytail that reached to his waist. He carried a sword upon his belt, and a shorter blade was tucked behind his back. His hair was white, and his face too was white with golden eyes. Rather than a tunic, he was clothed in a long white robe that covered his feet. His eyes met the eyes of the boy.

Daniel was not impressed by what he saw. Hagan seemed small and thin and weak compared to the other angels all around, though his sword was impressive. His wings were small, diminutive, almost as if they had been cut in half, and his eyes, though golden, did not have the same fiery glow as the others. Though angels were neither old nor young, Hagan just seemed to Daniel to be a little old and wore out. Even the white robe was slightly sloppy and out of place in this magnificent Valley of Eternity.

The boy wanted to ask Michael if he were sure this was the correct angel, but before he could say anything, Michael, spoke once again, "Valley of Eternity, Home of Angels, this is Daniel, son of David."

CHAPTER 2

One day prior

Michael and Uri were on the road to Jerusalem. It had been a while since Michael had been in Jerusalem, though he was not sure how long, as time had no real meaning to him.

Two days ago, he had been called by the Lord to enter into the Heavenly Realm, or as many angels referred to it, the "Throne of God," and he had bowed before the presence of the Lord of lords. The words spoken to him were in Enochian, the language of angels, and were clear and concise. Michael was to travel to Jerusalem and deliver a message to King David and his wife, Abigail. The message was that David's second son, Daniel, was to be given to the care of Michael and would be taken from his home, taken from David and Abigail, and given as a sacrifice into the care of angels. Michael bowed, head facing toward the ground and waited for the Lord to finish his message.

"Daniel is to be taken to the Valley of Eternity and delivered into the care of Hagan, of the third order, and will be taught and trained in the ways of the angel. No other word is needed at this time. Be prepared for battle, Michael, for there will certainly be resistance to your entrance into Jerusalem, and there will assuredly be battle. When you draw your sword and spread your wings and give your roar, remember, Michael, that the battle is mine." Michael felt the mist of God being unleashed upon him and felt the power and holiness fill into his inner being. The presence of the Lord suddenly was gone, and he felt himself being lifted by the seraphim and cherubim, heavenly creatures surrounding the throne of the Lord. Escorted out of the Heavenly Realm, Michael was clear on what was to be done. He did not ask nor consider why he had been requested for this task, yet he knew he was the chief of angels, and therefore, he knew the significance of this request from the Lord.

The road into Jerusalem was an ancient road used by men, angels, and demons for thousands of years. On the back of Pran, Michael could sense the presence of darkness and evil as he drew near to the gate of Jerusalem. Uri was by his side, atop his horse, and though his senses were not of the level of Michael, he too knew a spiritual battle was on the horizon. The men and women upon the road had no concept that they were in the presence of angels, for Michael and Uri were traveling in the spiritual dimension, unseen and unfelt by human beings around them.

Michael saw them first, a collection of demons lined in front of the gate. There must have been several hundred of them, reddish in color, in the form of men with wings made of a leathery substance, yet the heads were the heads of goats. Each had three eyes and two large horns that could move in any direction. Not all had tails coming from their backside, yet the ones in the front, the most powerful, had tails that could reach up to one hundred feet. All the demons had swords, blades blazing with fire, and the size of the demons was varied with the larger and more powerful in the front. None of the demons sat on horses as their wings kept them high above the human ground. As Michael saw the collection, he had no fear nor surprise, for fear was not a part of him, he was a defender angel, chief among warriors, and certainly the horde of demons in his pathway felt his presence of strength as he drew near. As Michael and Uri came within several feet of the demonic collection, the leader of the demons emerged to the front, and he was no stranger to Michael. Asmodeus stepped forward.

Asmodeus was a terrifying creature looking every bit like a monster of monsters. As Michael was to the angels, Asmodeus was to the demons. He had two heads, one like a bull and one like a man, his leathery wings larger even than the wings of Michael. He sat upon a lion with the wings and neck of a dragon. Two swords were connected to his waistband: one sword was Death and the other was Hell. His wings lifted him off his lion, and he walked several steps forward. Michael, lifting himself off Pran, walked several steps to stand face-to-face with Asmodeus.

"Greetings from the Lord of lords, Asmodeus," said Michael, to which Asmodeus replied, "Greetings from the Prince of the Earth, Michael." Asmodeus and Michael were similar in stature, both commanding a presence of strength and confidence. Although they had never actually met in battle, both reputations were well-known to the other. Neither felt fear of any kind. Asmodeus spoke, "You know, mighty warrior, that I cannot let you gain entrance into the city of Jerusalem, which belongs to and is under the dominion of my Lord, Lucifer. He has given me strict orders that your entrance is to be denied, and you will not come near the boy."

"I do not need your permission to enter the city. I come from the Lord and will complete the mission I am on," Michael replied.

Asmodeus drew Death and Hell and held them up to the sky with his arms raised. "You will not enter the city of Jerusalem. Death and Hell will remove the head of Michael if need be."

Michael took his right hand and brought it close to the hilt of his sword, Tyrfing, or "finger of God." Rarely did Michael draw this magnificent sword given to him by God himself to enable him to battle against Lucifer and his demons. To draw Tyrfing was equivalent to drawing the arm of God and was only done when God's power needed to be unleashed. Michael stared at Asmodeus and the other demons and knew there would be battle. "Uri, bring my shield and draw your sword, for we will fight this battle for the Lord." Uri brought the great shield with the emblem from God upon the front. It was a testament to Uri's strength that he could lift the mighty shield at all, much less carry it to Michael. The shield was grasped by the left hand of Michael, and with his right, the mighty Tyrfing slid from its scabbard.

Tyrfing was the most intimidating and devastating weapon anyone could lay eyes upon. It was huge and encircled with a light of blindness that would take away the sight of any demon gazing upon the blade itself. Fire came from its tip, lashing about like a tongue hungry for the blood of demons. When Michael held Tyrfing up in its glory, the demons felt true fear, for they were feeling the raw, unleashed power of God. The only demon not to take a few steps backward was Asmodeus. Death and Hell were swung in unison and hit down with full force upon the shield of Michael.

The fury of Michael burst forth with a scream that could be heard throughout the spiritual and heavenly realm. He blocked the blades of Death and Hell a second time with his shield and spun around, bringing the full force of Tyrfing upon the dual blades of Asmodeus. Followed by a second thrust at the blade of Hell, Hell fell out of the hand of the demon, and Tyrfing swung a backward blow looking for Death. Uri was fighting himself against many demons, blocking their thrusts and moving quick as lightning. Though not as big as Michael, Uri could handle himself against most any demon.

Michael and Asmodeus continued fighting, as the strength of Michael only increased the further the battle progressed. The horde of demons was trying to help Asmodeus, but the speed and power of Michael was too much for them to overcome. Suddenly, Asmodeus landed a blow to the back of Michael that knocked the mighty warrior off balance just slightly, but enough for a horde of demons to pounce on top of him. Uri screamed but could not reach him as he was having battle after battle with other demons. The redness of the demons grew in brightness, and demonic shrills screeched throughout the realm. The horns of Asmodeus moved downward like spears as he was ready to drive them into the neck of Michael. Out of the corner of his eye, Michael could see in a distance his brother, standing and gazing at the battle, an evil smile forming upon his mouth. His brother was Lucifer, the Prince of the Earth.

As the tips of the horns of Asmodeus touched the neck of Michael, Michael garnered all his holy strength, remembering that this battle was the Lord's, and threw the demons off him, knocking Asmodeus back. Michael brought the full force of Tyrfing down upon the wing of Asmodeus and knocked him sideways. Dropping his shield, he grabbed Asmodeus with his left arm, spun him toward him, and held him tightly, Tyrfing poised at both of his necks. Michael turned to look at his brother. Lucifer was well off into the distance, yet his voice was directly in front of Michael. "Nice fight, brother, it seems as if you have won this skirmish. Lucky for you I am not in the mood to take my brother's life right now. There will be another time for that. You may pass through the gate of Jerusalem, and you may encounter the boy, but rest assured, you and the boy will fall at my sword when the time is right."

Michael's left hand squeezed the neck of Asmodeus tighter. Taking Tyrfing to the throat of his second head, the head of a bull, Michael told him, "I am choosing to let you live this day, but you will no longer live with two heads." Tyrfing sliced through the neck of the bull head, removing it from the body of Asmodeus, who screamed from the depths of his evil being. Hundreds of demons were hissing, gnawing, and screeching. Lucifer, no longer smiling, was silent. He stared at Michael. After a moment, he spoke in Enochian, the language of the angels, "You and your worthless angels will fall for daring to challenge my kingdom. I know the plans of your meaningless God. The day is coming when you will face the wrath of the Prince of Darkness."

Michael let go of Asmodeus, looked toward Lucifer, and simply said, "I look forward to it, brother."

CHAPTER 3

David's palace was newly built as David had not resided in Jerusalem for long. Having been successful in conquering the Jebusites and capturing the city, David took up residence and called it the City of David. He had built up the city and the area around it, and he became more and more powerful because the Lord Almighty was with him. David had several wives, and he was the father to many sons and daughters. He brought several wives with him into the city of Jerusalem, and he added more once his residence was established in the royal city.

David loved each of his wives and made sure they had all that they needed. He was not able to spend as much time as he would have liked with each, as his duties as king seemed to grow with each passing day. The king had recently married Bathsheba. She had become his eighth wife, and David was madly in love with the dark-haired beauty. They had lost their first son during infancy, and both were hopeful for another child soon.

Uri stayed outside the royal palace, as Michael dismounted Pran and entered. Michael shape-shifted into the presence of a man; however, his angelic glow remained around him, and his presence was unmistakably that of an angel rather than a man. He glided directly past the guards into the chambers of the king, as David was preparing for his noonday meal. David immediately felt the warmth and presence as Michael entered unseen into the chambers. David turned and spoke, "Who is there? I can feel your presence." He immediately lied prostrate upon the ground. "Is it you, Lord?"

"Rise," Michael spoke. "I send you greetings from our Lord." David slowly rose to his feet, and suddenly Michael appeared to him. He saw a mighty warrior, close to seven feet tall, with long flowing hair and piercing eyes. The sword hung loosely to his side, and no wings were evident since Michael was in the form of a man. David was not a man used to feeling fear. He was favored by God and had won great victories, being blessed by the hand of God time and again. He had conquered giants, killed lions, destroyed bears, and seen the hand of God fight for him. However, he had never felt as he felt in the presence of Michael the archangel. David knew he was in the company of something mighty, and he fell prostrate to the ground again. To which Michael replied, "I have spoken to rise, now rise to your feet, son of God, and hear the word of the Lord. I am not to be worshipped. I am the bringer of news from the Lord." Michael spoke with an air of authority and forcefulness, although delivering messages to men was not what he was normally called upon to do. Gabriel normally received the messenger tasks. For reasons known only to God himself, though, Michael was the chosen one for this special message. David rose.

"I am here to take something from you," Michael said. "The Lord requires of you a son to be handed over to myself. This son will travel to the Valley of Eternity, to be trained as an angel, to learn the ways of the angel, to live among the angels. He will be under the tutelage of Hagan, master defender and master of swords. Your son will become a great defender, a great warrior. Do not ask me if you will ever see your son again, for that is not in my knowledge nor is it proper for me to speculate."

Michael spoke in Enochian, the angelic dialect, yet David heard the words in Hebrew. "My son is to become an angel?"

"Not become an angel. I did not say he would become an angel. He will be trained in the ways of the angel. He will learn the language of angels and the battle techniques of angels and the thought process of angels. He will not become an angel. He will become a great defender."

David was mesmerized by the voice of Michael, and he did not know how to respond. He finally said, "Am I to choose which son?" Immediately after he spoke, he realized how silly he sounded, how naïve he was being thinking that he would choose the son. David corrected himself at once. "Tell me which of my sons the Lord requires," he said. David had six sons born to him in Hebron, prior to him becoming king of Israel. His sons born in Hebron were Amnon, Daniel, Absalom, Adonijah, Shephatiah, and Ithream. Since he had been established in Jerusalem, he had become the father of Shammua, Shobab, and Nathan. Nine sons had been born to him so far, and surely many more would follow. These sons had been born to him by seven wives, and in his mind, he quickly attempted to guess the name of the son who would become the defender.

His guess was his firstborn, Amnon, who seemed about the right age to be trained. David did not have a close relationship with any of his sons born to him in Hebron. He had not spent much time with them, as he was constantly at war. One of the aspects of his life God had placed upon his heart was to become a better father and to really develop a relationship with his sons.

Michael spoke, "The son who will travel with me to the Valley of Eternity is Daniel, son of Abigail." David's heart hurt immediately. This was his second born son and was most certainly the son that favored him the most. How old was Daniel, David thought, he must be eleven or twelve years of age by now? Abigail will most certainly be crushed. Daniel, who Abigail liked to call Chileab, was her only child. Abigail was David's third wife and was a good woman. In fact, David wanted to find more time to spend with her. She had a calming presence about her and was undoubtedly the most spiritual of David's wives. Daniel and Abigail were inseparable, but the Lord had spoken. "Tell me what to do," David said to Michael. "You are to go and speak to the boy's mother. Bring the boy here tomorrow by noon. We will depart at that time." Michael was gone as he disappeared from the chamber. David took a deep breath, got down on his knees, and spoke this prayer to the Lord:

Great are you Lord, and worthy of praise.
You are to be feared among all the Gods.
Splendor and majesty are before you, Strength and
*   majesty are all about you.*
I worship the splendor of your holiness.
Let the heavens rejoice, let the earth be glad,
Let the sea resound, and all that is in it,
For you are righteous.
You make my enemies tremble before me,
You fight my enemies and lift me up in victory.
May you take my son, and may you bless him as you
*   have blessed me.*
May you make him into a great defender, a great
*   defender for you, and a great defender of your*
*   people.*
May your power, and your strength, and your holi-
*   ness, be planted deep within him.*
Amen.

David walked to the home of Abigail. It sat on a hilltop just a short distance from the palace. David had spoken to no one about what must be done, and he was accompanied only by his household guards. He politely knocked at the door to the home, and Abigail's handmaiden, Lizona, opened the door. She bowed before the king. David heard the sound of a harp being played, recognized the song, and smiled in his heart, asking Lizona if it was Daniel playing. She replied, "Yes, my lord, he is performing his daily lessons under the teaching of Josephus."

"Take me to him," David instructed.

Lizona led him through the hallways to the stairway, and they climbed to the third floor of the home. The king entered the room, and Daniel and Josephus both bowed, one knee upon the floor. "Greetings, Josephus, and greetings, my son. You are obviously doing a tremendous job teaching Daniel the chords and notes of the harp. Well done," said David.

"Thank you, my king, he is a natural, and it comes easily to him. These moments with him are the most joyous part of my days."

"I have some things to discuss with my son and his mother. You may say your farewell to Daniel, thank you for all you have done," David said.

Josephus stood and thought to himself how strangely the king had told him to say farewell to Daniel. It almost sounded as if he would not see the boy for a while. He hugged Daniel and looked him in the eye, saying, "Goodbye, my young pupil, you have almost mastered the harp, the sound of beauty flows from your hands."

Daniel replied, "I will see you tomorrow, Josephus, and I will try to work on 'In the Fields of Ancient Days.'" David handed him a golden coin as he left the room and said, "Thank you again, good friend, for teaching my son, I am honored Abigail chose you to instruct him. Until we meet again."

David walked over to Daniel and gave him an awkward hug. He picked up the harp of Josephus and asked Daniel if he would play "In the Fields of Ancient Days" with him. "I will do my best,

Father," Daniel said, and he positioned his hands upon his harp. The king began the chords and immediately he and Daniel were playing. Daniel matching David chord for chord. Abigail heard the beautiful sound and, instantly, knew who had come. For there was none in all the land who could play the harp like David, and it was one of the traits she most admired about him.

He could fight with sword, lead men into battle, and also play beautiful music on the harp. Abigail was determined that Daniel would follow in his father's footsteps. None of David's other sons were required to learn the harp and, instead, spent most of their time learning the art of warfare and studying the written histories of famous battles. Daniel would be different, Abigail had decided, and would become both a warrior and musician.

Abigail hurried to the third floor, entered the room, and saw father and son side by side playing the beautiful melody. She had never seen such a beautiful sight nor heard such a beautiful sound, both father and son, eyes closed, playing in unison as if the heavens themselves were bowed before them. In the fields of ancient days, upon the green meadows of Israel long ago, peaceful shepherds sung their songs and played their harps… Abigail could see that David was crying as he played. It was a moment Abigail would cherish in her heart in the long, lonely days that were about to befall her.

The music stopped. David, cheeks covered with tears, said, "Daniel, you are a far greater harpist than I, and I am proud of you."

"Thank you, Father. I can only hope to become as great of a musician as you one day."

The king replied, "Let me speak alone with your mother at this time, I will see you again momentarily. Go to your room and wait for me there." As Daniel left the room, Abigail sensed something was wrong. "He is a fine boy," David said, "you have done an outstanding job with him."

"I have missed you. I have not seen you in several weeks. Is everything okay, my lord king?" Abigail asked.

"Yes, everything is fine, I apologize for not seeing you for some time, you and Daniel have been in my thoughts and prayers. I just seem to be pulled in a thousand different directions. I know that I need to spend more time with all my family. I appreciate everything you have done with Daniel, but there is something urgent that must be discussed between us." The king continued, "I had a visitor today during the noontime."

David did not know how to break the news to Abigail, so he just took a deep breath and started to speak. He told her of Michael and the message from the Lord, that Daniel would leave with Michael and be taken to the Valley of Eternity to be raised and trained by the angels. "I know that this is hard for you to hear, but please consider it a great honor that our son has been chosen by God for this special task. He will be in the hands of the Lord and his angels. *Jehovah Jireh,* the Lord will provide."

Abigail was frozen; tears would not stop flowing from her eyes. "No, no, no," was all that would come out. Daniel was her life, her only child, her world. She was far from her home, the king rarely had time for her, and she knew in her heart of hearts she would conceive no more children. This could not possibly be from God. "This is not from the Lord. I cannot allow this to happen! Please, David, please, do not allow this to occur. Do not let him take our son!" Abigail walked toward the king and started pounding on his chest. More tears until finally Abigail collapsed at the feet of David.

David had no words. He knew the total despair deep within the heart of Abigail. Prayer came from his lips, "Lord, please provide for Abigail, touch her spirit and her soul and her heart. Provide for her. Let her rest in your peace and in your strength. May she trust in your goodness and your mercy, and may she trust that this is from you." Abigail stood up, looked into the eyes of David, and said, "I am going with him. We will be ready within the hour." David touched her shoulders and said, "No, my Abigail. This is a path that Daniel must travel without you. You may come with him to my palace and see him off, but Michael was clear the boy would travel alone with him and his armorbearer." David continued, "I know how hard this is for you, my sweet Abigail, yet I also know of your goodness and your love for God, and I know that He will comfort you. Now, go get Daniel and let us be on our way."

Daniel did not exactly know what was happening. He was only told that he would spend the night with his father and mother in the king's palace before embarking on a long trip the following day. He was told to bring just a few items of clothing but nothing else, not even his harp. His mother would not stop hugging him and telling him how much she loved him. His father was quietly stoic as he led the way to the palace. It seemed to Daniel as if they were somehow telling him goodbye, and he felt a strange empty feeling in his stomach. Next morning, his world would change forever.

Abigail lay with eyes wide open. It was the middle of the night, her last night with her son. Her mind kept drifting back to when she first met David as he traveled to her home in Carmel. Although married to Nabal at the time, she had feelings for David from the moment she laid eyes on him. He was a good man. A righteous man. A man who tried to do the right things. She told herself that she must trust him. Must trust the Lord. She would have to let him go.

She got up, tiptoed quietly to Daniel's room in the palace. Walking to where he lay sleeping, she stood over him, staring at the young boy who looked so much like his father. *My little Chileab*, she thought. She prayed over him. "Lord, I do not know what this is all about. I am heartbroken and full of anxiousness. You know how much I love my son. I ask that you protect wherever you may lead him. Keep him from harm and grow him into a man who yearns after you and your ways. Help him to have a hunger and a thirst for righteousness. Lord, I do not even know what a defender is, but whatever it is, may you make my son into the greatest defender he could possibly be. May he always know his mother loves him, amen."

She gently crawled into the bed with him. She put her hand upon his chest and lay there feeling the beating of his heart. Her eyes were wet, her heart was heavy, and her soul was burdened as she finally drifted off to sleep.

Breakfast was served, followed by the midmorning ritual of King David standing on his balcony and waving to the people of Jerusalem. The people would gather outside the palace each day, hoping to receive a wave and a smile from the king of whom they loved. David performed the ritual and outwardly put on his usual air of confidence and strength, yet inside, his heart was broken. He was more broken for Abigail than for Daniel. He knew that God would protect and provide for his son, but he was worried for Abigail. How would she handle the departure? How would she react to living without her son? Would she hold it against him? Would their relationship ever be the same?

It was just a few minutes before the noon hour and David, Abigail, and Daniel stood inside the king's chamber, each staring at the door. At precisely noon, Michael appeared, looking exactly as he had looked the previous day. At first, only David and Daniel could see him. Daniel was in complete awe and shock. He had never seen anything as powerful as this huge, bright heavenly creature. "Greetings, David and Daniel," said Michael. "Are you ready for the journey?" Daniel just simply nodded. His father and mother had told him early this morning that he would be going on a journey with an angel from heaven. They told him they loved him and were proud of him. They did not know when they would see him again but asked that he be obedient to the angels and listen to all they would say to him.

Abigail spoke to Michael, "I cannot see you. I wish to see who is taking my son from me. Please, I ask in the name of the Lord, let my eyes see you, Michael." Michael appeared to Abigail, and she was in complete silence as she looked upon this huge angel in the form of a man. She saw his strength and his light surrounding him as her eyes met his golden, piercing gaze. It took all the courage she could muster as she spoke to Michael, "I would like to travel with my son, to accompany him and to learn the ways of the angel as well." David turned and looked at her, but she kept her gaze firmly focused upon the angel.

Michael looked at the grief-stricken mother and spoke, "I have been instructed by our Lord to travel with only the boy. He will be in good hands and be taken care of in the safety of the Valley of Eternity. I cannot allow your request, as it goes against my instructions. However, I will allow you to see my full glory and to see my full strength and my full presence before we depart."

Michael became his full angelic being directly in front of David, Daniel, and Abigail. The archangel in his full glory, wings expanded, tunic draped tightly, and Tyrfing hanging upon his waist. Neither David nor Abigail had ever seen something so magnificent, so majestic. Pran walked up to Michael, and Uri was already on his horse, also in full glory. "It is time," Michael said. Abigail turned to Daniel, "I love you, my Chileab, may the Lord guard your paths, and may we see each other again." David simply placed his two hands on the cheeks of Daniel, and said, "Goodbye, my son. May you find favor with the Lord. Jehovah-Jireh." Daniel walked toward Michael, was picked up by his mighty right hand, and placed behind him on Pran. David and Abigail gazed heavenward as their son and angels disappeared from their sight. Neither was sure they would ever see their son again.

CHAPTER 4

Daniel was not sure how long it had taken to arrive at the mighty gate. On the one hand, it seemed as if they had just left Jerusalem, while, on the other, it seemed as if they had been traveling for weeks. It was a strange sensation to feel as if time did not exist, and Daniel was in a definite state of confusion. He was lonely and already missed his mother, yet he could feel the comfort pouring out from the trees as they walked on the air through the valley.

Daniel was in midair in the center of the angelic beings, high above the river. "Valley of Eternity, home of angels, this is Daniel, son of David."

Michael carried Daniel to the top of the tree of trees and set him down upon the branches. Daniel believed he would fall straight to the bottom of the tree; however, he stood on the branches as he would a wooden floor. He felt secure and safe as he looked and saw an angel in a long robe approaching. This was the angel called Hagan, and again, Daniel noticed how different he was from Michael. He was tall and thin with wings that were much smaller but seemed to move a little faster. "My archangel," Hagan spoke as he settled in the top of the tree. "Greetings, Hagan. It is an honor for me to present you with Daniel, son of David. He will be in your primary care as the Lord has chosen you with the honor of training him in the ways of the angel."

"I do thank our Lord for the honor," replied Hagan, "yet I cannot help but question why I have been assigned this task. There are many more qualified than I."

Michael responded, "It is not for us to question the Lord. It is only for us to obey and to accept the tasks which we have been given. I know that this is your first assignment since the failure. Perhaps the Lord is providing redemption and allowing you to fully return to the angel you were created to be. Your teaching skills are superior, and your swordsmanship exceeds all of the angels in your realm. Mold and shape young Daniel into the great defender he must become. Let not this opportunity go to waste."

"Yes, my archangel, I am thankful for you and for the Lord. I will begin immediately," Hagan said as he took hold of Daniel and, together, they flew through the valley to a tall tree in the middle of the eastern bank.

Daniel held on tight to the hand of Hagan as they flew into the top of the tree and seemed to continue deeper and deeper until the branches finally subsided. It was as if they were traveling inside a long circular cave until it emptied out into an open area full of light. There was no floor, yet as Daniel let go of the hand of Hagan, he felt as though he were standing on solid ground. Hagan said, "Do not worry, young Daniel, this is the heart of the tree where much of our training will take place. You are safe here and are to feel no fear. You must have many questions for me about your new home, but first, you must gather some rest. This will be the area where you sleep. You will simply lie down, and the tree will provide you some form of darkness to which you are accustomed. I will have food and clothing for you when you awake." Hagan was gone. Daniel stood for a long time because he did not know how he could lie down in midair. Finally, he acted as if he were climbing into a loft and lay down. He felt supported and comfortable and very tired. Before he drifted off to sleep, Daniel thought of his mother and father and said a prayer that God would watch over them. He fell asleep humming the song

"In the Fields of Ancient Days," as he imagined he and his father together again playing the chords as one.

"Routine, routine, routine!" Hagan was bellowing throughout the chamber where Daniel was waking up. "It is all about routine. The way of the angel is all about the way of order and routine and consistency. Rise up and put this on, we must be at the table immediately." Daniel took the white robe, placed it over his head, and let it fall to his ankles. He ran after Hagan as fast as he could, barely grabbing hold of his robe and flying out the heart of the tree into the branches and out into the open area of the valley. There in the middle of the river sat an enormous table, filled with angels. Thousands of angels. Hagan led Daniel to a specific area, and they sat down.

Angels were speaking in a language Daniel had never heard, many of them directing questions to Hagan. Suddenly, a huge tablecloth fell out of the sky and covered the table. On the tablecloth was food placed directly in front of each angel. The food was a fine, flake-like wafer that had a rose-like smell to it. Daniel picked his up, placed it in his mouth and was startled at how sweet it tasted. It tasted like wafers made with honey. As Daniel ate one, another appeared. He ate three before feeling the sensation of a full stomach. Hagan leaned into him and said, "That is what we call manna. The food of angels. You will eat manna once a day, and it will sustain you and keep you healthy. You will require no other food and will grow tall and strong. We will drink the water from the river during the evening. Your body will begin to change, you will see."

"Where do I, well, where do I go, you know, to the bathroom?" Daniel asked Hagan.

"That too will end. Your body will not be under the law of physics anymore. But for now, we will go to the southwestern edge of the gate," Hagan answered. Daniel had no idea what Hagan was talking about; all he knew was he needed to use the bathroom.

Ishboth was pulling the gate open as angels flew out of the Valley of Eternity. "Where are they going?" asked Daniel.

"Each angel has specific assignments that they perform each day." Hagan continued, "Depending on the realm to which they belong, the tasks are different and involve different areas of expertise. Each task varies, and some take longer than others. All angels receive their assignments from the leader of their realm, and all angels know the exact moment the gate will be open and when the gate will be shut. You see that cluster of trees, down close to the edge of the gate? You may walk there and relieve yourself."

Daniel returned, and Hagan could tell he had been thinking about some of the things he had learned so far. "What realm do you belong to, Hagan?"

"I belong to the Defender Realm, and so will you. Our task is to defend the people of the Lord whenever need be," Hagan explained.

"Do all angels in the Defender Realm look like you?" Daniel really did not think Hagan looked like much of a warrior.

Hagan chuckled, "No, in fact, no two angels look the same. We are all created by the Lord in different shapes and sizes. We are not young and are not old and do not age."

"Am I going to turn into an angel?" Daniel asked.

"No, son, you are definitely a human being, but you will develop many angelic characteristics, and you will undergo certain changes in your physical appearance that will be considered angel-ic-like. Probably, the best way I could describe it to you is that you will become half-angel, half-human."

That sounded like the craziest thing Daniel had ever heard, but he let it go because Hagan had lifted him up and said, "Now it is time to begin training."

Daniel did not know exactly where they were but felt like it was somewhere close to Hagan's "angel tree headquarters." It was an open area, and there were angels all around practicing with swords, and some were using bows and arrows. Walking among the angels were several dressed exactly like Hagan, with long white robes, hair falling down their backs, smaller, quicker wings coming out of their shoulders. Daniel knew right away that these angels were all about business as their voices resonated higher and more powerfully than he had heard so far. He still could not tell what they were saying. It sounded like some form of faraway language. "When do I get my sword?" asked Daniel.

"Oh, we are a long, long way from that, boy. You must first gain strength," Hagan responded. "Strength is the key for you to being able to lift and maneuver the angel's sword. Your body must be trained and must become machine-like before we advance to the next stage of training. We will call this the foundation training."

Hagan led Daniel to an area where there were no other angels, only what appeared to be stumps of trees. The stumps were in all different shapes and sizes, and there must have been at least fifty scattered throughout the area. "When you can lift each of these stumps twenty times above your head, you will be ready to graduate to the next form of training," said Hagan. Daniel just stared at him. "Get busy, boy, they are not going to lift themselves."

Daniel lost track of the days or the weeks or the months as he began his training. It must have taken him a month before he could even lift one stump one time above his head. He worked on his technique each training session and soon noticed his body growing slowly in stature and strength. He lost all concept of time, as the only thing that mattered to him was lifting angel tree stumps over his head day after day.

He began to piece together bits and pieces of the Enochian language spoken by the angels. It helped when other angels came to his "stump field" to watch him or talk to him. Daniel sat mesmerized one day as an angel named Bildad lifted each stump fifty times over his head without as much as struggling for even one rep. "How did you do that?" To which Bildad responded, "You must remember, young Daniel, that we are created with our angelic strength. It has been given to us by the Lord. You must develop your strength. Do not be discouraged, for I can see how you continue to improve."

Daniel spent most of his time around other angels in the Defender Realm. Hagan was right when he explained how each angel was not only different in appearance but also had his own unique personality. Though no angel ever showed any outward emotion, all had unique characteristics that Daniel began to pick up on. There was Bildad, who was always quick to demonstrate things to Daniel and came to see him more than any other. Gad was another angel who helped him more than the others as far as learning the language. He would playfully slap Daniel across the head when he misspoke a word or did not know the meaning of certain words and phrases. Mahlon allowed Daniel to watch him work the sword over and over. In Daniel's mind, Mahlon was the best angel he had seen with the sword. He was so quick and so graceful, it was hard for the other angels in the Defender Realm to keep up with Mahlon. One day, Daniel mentioned to Hagan how great he thought Mahlon was with the sword, to which Hagan responded, "He is okay. I have seen many far greater than he."

Daniel muttered under his breath, "I don't know about that."

Hagan turned and looked at Daniel directly in the eyes and said, "Do not be mesmerized or intimidated by them. You will become far greater than all of them. Perhaps one day I will show you a thing or two about the sword. But first, you have some stumps to lift."

CHAPTER 5

Lucifer, the Prince of the Earth, hovered high above Namok located in the first atmosphere above the Earth. Sometimes referred to as hell, Namok was the home of demons and spirits of the damned. A place of darkness and punishment and decomposition, Namok was marked as the abode of unquenchable fire. Lucifer's home, his creation, was born after a rebellion had occurred in heaven and one-third of the angels had been cast out of the Valley of Eternity. To be trapped inside the gates of Namok was to be in a prison full of complete darkness with suffering, torture, and eternal separation from God.

It had become the custom for some of the inhabitants of Earth to call him Satan, yet he insisted his demons call him by his angelic name of Lucifer, which means "star of the morning." His princely kingdom had begun with the rebellion in the Valley of Eternity. However, the rebellion had not gone exactly as Lucifer had hoped.

Lucifer had grown tired of sharing power with his archangelic brother, Michael. He had begun to feel a tinge of jealousy toward his brother, who he felt was favored by the Lord. Both he and Michael possessed exquisite beauty, great wisdom, and mighty power, and both shared positions of enormous influence as they were considered the guardian archangels of the Valley of Eternity. Wickedness, jealousy, and impurity had begun to creep into the spirit of Lucifer. Created and designed by God for holiness, he began to feel the lure and the temptation and the belief that he was on equal terms with the

Lord. Lucifer became prideful because of his beauty, and his splendor and strength became the root of his corruption.

He could no longer resist the lust and the desire for more. Lucifer wanted to be worshipped. His plan was to become greater than God. He gathered many angels in the valley and began to promote himself, saying, "I will ascend into heaven, I will exalt my throne above the stars of God. I will ascend above the heights of the clouds, I will be like the Most High." He knew he had his followers and had been personally recruiting angels he considered to be pivotal to his rebellion. The one angel he needed and had been trying to convince to follow him was Hagan, the master of swords, Defender of Defenders. The showdown between Lucifer and God was inevitable, and as it drew closer, he was relentless in his recruitment of Hagan. Lucifer knew that he would soon stand before the Lord and declare his equality and demand his rightful throne. He made one last pitch to Hagan. "Come with me, Hagan, you will be my Defender Angel, second only to myself. You will be placed above all others. Your sword, Breather of Life, will be the sword all will bow to and all will submit to." Lucifer continued, "I need you, for there is no angelic being that can match you in a fight, except for myself and Michael. Come, let us ascend to the throne together, let us rule and let us absorb and soak the power that is rightfully ours!" The words were persuasive, and Hagan eventually bowed the knee to Lucifer.

The morning came, and the Lord's presence descended into the Valley of Eternity. The voice of the Lord, speaking in Enochian, vibrated throughout the valley. "Lucifer, come stand in my presence." Lucifer, with Asmodeus and Hagan standing directly behind him, flew into the cloud of the presence of the Lord. The Lord spoke: "Lucifer, star of the morning, I know your desires and I know your lust and I know your jealousy. You have come to believe you can be an equal to me, but you are wrong. Your desires will only lead you to become a thief, a killer, and a destroyer. You will not ascend to the heights of heaven, for you are being banished. You and your followers are hereby thrown from heaven and banished from the Valley of Eternity."

Lightning crashed. Thunder rolled. The whirlwind picked up speed. Lucifer and his followers, close to one-third of the angels in the valley, were caught up in the whirlwind and thrust into the darkness, falling and falling until, ultimately, they landed in Namok, the atmosphere above the Earth. The last thing Hagan remembered was gazing into the eyes of Michael before he was swept up.

Cast from heaven, Lucifer and his followers heard the voice of the Lord again immediately as they landed into the desolation that was Namok. "You are fallen angels. I know that you will tempt, taunt, tease, deceive, afflict, and accuse the people of Earth. But you have no power to physically harm my people. You are not to lay a hand nor thrust a sword at any of my followers. Your final defeat is already written, and your ultimate destruction has already been determined. You and your dominions may have charge of the Earth for a period but know that the day is fast approaching when your fate will be permanently cast." Silence.

Lucifer could still hear those words, and they tormented him. Asmodeus, scarred and one-headed, arrived. Lucifer said, "The boy took me by surprise. I am sure he is under the tutelage of Hagan. We must speed up the process of the destruction of King David. He must not be allowed to father any more sons. If we act now, we can destroy the line of David and what is to come from it."

Asmodeus responded, "I believe Rapha is ready with his sons. There is no power on Earth that can stop them. They are able to do the work we are not allowed to do. They will strike and kill the king and any that stand in their way. You have done a wonderful job, Lucifer, with Rapha. He is thirsty for blood and will do whatever you command. You are his Lord."

The demons in Namok were restless, for they knew a great battle was brewing. Rapha, the giant of giants, and his sons were about to rampage.

CHAPTER 6

Hagan knew immediately as he fell out of the Valley of Eternity, he had made a huge mistake. But it was too late. He had begun to travel down a path for which there was no return. He felt weakened somehow when he arrived in Namok, although his outward strength and glory remained on full display. Hagan was tremendous in size, and muscles bulged from his legs to his arms. Golden armbands were wrapped tight around his wrists, and his wings were a golden feathery material that were also huge in scope. His movements were graceful, and no angel or demon would ever want to face the wrath of the sword of Hagan, Breather of Life. He wore angelic battle armor made from bronze, and it emanated a glow. He had been created by the Lord to be a warrior, a symbol of strength, a defender of the faith. His power was second only to Michael and Lucifer. But once he had been cast from the valley, all he felt was loneliness.

Hagan was snapped out of his memory of Namok by Daniel, watching the young boy as he moved from stump to stump lifting and lifting, pressing each high above his head. Although he had not really been paying attention, his spirit being elsewhere, far away and a long time ago, Hagan now looked at Daniel, and he took note how the boy had gained noticeable size and strength since his arrival in the valley. He was no longer a "little boy" but had grown into a tall and strong young man. He could now lift every stump and press the required number of repetitions high above his head. He could speak the language, although Gad was still quick to slap his head over even a minor mishap.

Daniel had no idea how long he had been in the valley as there was no concept of time, no keeper of days, and no method to mark the passage of months. *Was Hagan even paying attention to me?* thought Daniel. *I have done nothing but lift and lift. I have never even touched a sword, and I have definitely never seen Hagan even draw his from the scabbard.* Daniel was beginning to doubt if Hagan even knew how to fight. Perhaps Michael had assigned the wrong angel to train him. As Daniel was thinking about how he could find Michael to ask for a new trainer, Hagan suddenly glided and stood directly in front of him. "You have done well, boy. Your strength training is complete, and you now have the necessary size and strength to move onto the next phase of your development. As soon as I receive permission, we will move to the next phase which will include the usage and techniques of angelic swordsmanship. Now, go and watch the others but stay completely out of the way." Hagan was gone.

Daniel remained frustrated. As usual, he did not fully comprehend what Hagan was trying to say to him. Mahlon was flying toward the training area when Daniel waved him to come toward him. "Can you answer a question for me, Mahlon?"

"If I am able," replied Mahlon.

Daniel told him about Hagan and his words, "As soon as I receive permission."

"If Hagan is supposed to be training me and I am ready to learn the art of the sword, why would he need permission to begin that part of the training?" asked Daniel.

"Daniel, there is part of Hagan which you do not understand. I cannot fully explain it to you, you will have to speak with him directly. But I can tell you what every angel knows. Hagan is not allowed to draw his sword from his scabbard without permission from the Lord God himself."

That was puzzling. Why would Hagan need permission in order to draw his sword? Daniel wondered why he would even be allowed to carry a sword if he could not draw it. What kind of warrior teacher could not pull his own sword from the scabbard?

Mahlon finished his answer by stating, "As far as I can ever remember, I have never seen Hagan pull his sword. They say it has the name Breather of Life, but I cannot speak on it as I have never seen it."

Daniel thanked Mahlon and made a note to himself to ask Hagan about his sword. There was a mystery to Hagan that Daniel could not seem to unlock. He would speak to others and was not standoffish, yet there was almost something sad about him, and it seemed to Daniel that Hagan's presence was often far away in another place, lonely.

Rapha was a giant. He was eight feet tall and weighed a full 450 pounds. There was not an inch of fat on his body; he was completely made of muscle. His hair was long, and his face had never been shaved. A long flowing black beard made his menacing presence even more intimidating. No one could look upon Rapha and not feel total fear. He had been born in a Mediterranean coast city south of Tyre called Haifa. Nobody knew the age of Rapha or his three sons, only that they were all equally imposing and had seemingly been around forever. What they wanted, they took; what they did not like, they killed; and what they wanted to do, they simply did. There was no mercy nor kindness of any sort. Rapha's three sons were named Saph, Lahmi, and Ishbi and were famous for their cruelty and ruthlessness.

Rapha never knew his father nor his mother, but he had heard tales of his mom and her black-haired beauty. He did not remember the morning the demon angels came, taking him away from his home, away from his mother, to a faraway place full of anger, fire, and demons. He was sure his mother had cried hysterically as her son was taken from her. As hard as Rapha used to try, he could never find a memory of his home or mother or father, and he eventually stopped trying as he was indoctrinated in the way of the demon and filled with hatred and anger and brutality. He was not sure what ever became of his true family, and after many years, he did not care anymore.

His first kill had been an entire family of travelers making a pilgrimage to the city of Jerusalem. With no remorse, he had drawn his sword, slit the five throats, and taken the wagon and all their belongings. With every kill came a thirst for more. He became accustomed to hearing the small whisper of the demon in his spirit urging him to rape, kill, and destroy. His first rape had resulted in a son, Saph, of whom the demons demanded be turned over to them for the demonic indoctrination. Another rape produced Lahmi, and yet another bore his third and final son, Ishbi. Lahmi and Ishbi, like Saph, were fully immersed and trained in the way of the demonic angel. All worshipped Lucifer and were sworn to do his bidding.

The love was withdrawn from their hearts and their spirits, as they were taught to kill, hate, and destroy. Namok had been the home of Rapha during his youth and indoctrination. Lucifer became the father he had never known. The demons were his brothers. When he was permitted to finally leave Namok and live upon the earth, he was completely devoted to the ways of evil. Each of his sons had also been forced to live in Namok until Lucifer decided that they could be trusted to live on the earth and carry out his demonic wishes.

The giants had participated in many wars through the years. They fought side by side with Amorites, Hittites, and the Philistines. Whether they were on the winning side or the losing side, one thing was certain when the giants fought—blood would be shed, and bodies ripped open, and enemies by the thousands brutalized. They fought not to win victories but rather to satisfy their insatiable lust for blood and inhumanity. Lucifer was like a proud father watching Rapha and his sons seek and destroy lives. They were killing machines who killed whatever and whoever Lucifer ordered. The order that would change the path of the world was about to be revealed to Rapha.

"Greetings, Rapha," said Lucifer as he and Asmodeus approached. "How are you and your sons?"

"We are fine, a little restless for some battle, but otherwise we are fine," responded Rapha. "Do you have a task for us?"

"Yes," said Lucifer. "I need you to send a message to the king of Israel and Judah, his name is David, son of Jesse, born in Bethlehem."

Daniel was sparring with Bildad. He was mirroring every move although the sword he was using felt way too heavy for him. It never seemed fair for him as he worked with the angels because he could never seem to gain an advantage since the angels simply used their wings to lift and move themselves around, while Daniel could only turn and react. Hagan would be yelling, "Move! Attack! Balance!" His favorite line was always "Control your spirit!" Hagan would have Daniel work with different angels every day, and he soon learned that each had their own unique style. Some were fast and graceful, others were full of strength and power, while others fought defensively. "Learn something every session and combine all the different styles into your own. Do not ever settle for being good at only a few things. Be the complete warrior, one who can fight any style against any opponent."

"I don't see how I will ever be able to fight against other angels without the ability to fly. It is too big of an advantage," Daniel said to Hagan after one particular brutal session against an angel named

Pilfer. Pilfer had been all over Daniel, flying all around and hitting him again and again with the side of his sword. Daniel felt he would have died a hundred times if it had been a real fight. "You must control your spirit and only worry about that which you can control. You must master your movement and learn when to attack and when to react. Why do you say that you cannot fly?" asked Hagan.

Daniel was stunned, "Uh, because it is pretty obvious, I have no wings. I am sure everyone can look at me and know I am not an angel."

"Interesting," was all Hagan replied.

After a long silence, Hagan looked deeply into Daniel's eyes and spoke words that Daniel would never forget. "I have told you that you are no longer under the laws of physics. Yes, it helps to have wings because they provide precision in movement and the ability to fly and attack at different speeds. But you will fly, Daniel, even with no wings, you will fly, because I will teach you. But first, you must learn to stop focusing on what you cannot do and instead focus on all that you can do. Once your spirit is in complete balance, there will be no warrior, be it man or angel, that will be able to defeat you."

The training continued. The sword grew lighter. The moves came easier. The beatdowns were fewer. Hagan had begun sparring himself with Daniel, albeit with no sword. The entire focus was on movement. Daniel would be required to match Hagan move for move, mirroring every arm, leg, shoulder, or head movement. Daniel had to admit that he was impressed with Hagan. He had seen no angel move with such precision and quickness. It was as if he was always many moves ahead of Daniel, moving with an air of authority and supremacy. "Control your spirit, feel your opponent, know his strengths and weaknesses!"

As the movement sparring sessions continued, Daniel began to grow in confidence. Hagan could feel his confidence rising and pushed him harder and harder. During one particular session, Daniel seemed to be in a trance as he matched Hagan move for move. He did not notice the eyes gathering and watching. Angels of the Defender Realm had gathered to watch this young human-angel matching the famed Hagan move for move. They saw not a young boy any longer, but rather, a strong young man who had learned to move like an angel. What they saw was Daniel, and he was flying!

Throughout the Valley of Eternity, Hagan could not shake Daniel. They eventually settled before the Tree of Trees. It was then that Daniel realized what he had done. "How did I just do that, Hagan? How was I able to fly? I have no wings," Daniel asked his trainer.

"Your body is different than an angel's body. Your mindset is different too. You can do things an angel cannot do. Once your mind is in total balance with your body, and you are totally focused on your opponent, you need no ground to stand on, you need only your mind. Let gravity exit your thoughts, let limitations exit, let the concept of legs and feet and walking exit. All your purpose, all your metaphysical focus, all your energy must be on your opponent. It is then that you can redefine what you can and cannot do. You become one with your opponent, and you know what he is going to do before he does it. Your mind has the ability to sense and feel and know when an opponent is about to strike. It is not that you are flying. You are simply moving." As Hagan finished speaking, Daniel was totally confused and was not sure exactly what he had heard, but he had no time to process it. The archangel Michael had appeared.

Michael was absolutely magnificent as he stood in front of Hagan and Daniel. He was the very definition of power and authority. Daniel had not seen him in some time, but his appearance had not changed. His wings were huge and spread, his eyes golden and piercing, his sword, Tyrfing, huge, and his hair was flowing down his back. He did not smile nor show any emotion at all. "You have done well so far, Daniel. I encourage you to continue to learn the ways of the Defender. It is my belief that our Lord has mighty plans for you," Michael's voice bellowed out in the Enochian dialect. Daniel understood him but was unable to speak, his mouth would not even open; in fact, he found himself staring down. Hagan spoke, "My archangel Michael, I believe it is time to move to the next stage of training for Daniel. He has been using swords and has been learning certain battle movements and techniques, however, for me to impart upon him the full knowledge of the Defender, I believe I must draw Breather of Life and teach him the way of the Lord's Sword. I know I must receive permission before drawing the sword, and so I am asking permission at this time."

Michael stared at Hagan. It was as if he knew the sword had not been drawn in an exceptionally long time and wanted to say something about it. Instead, his only reply was, "Thank you for your request, Hagan. I will take it to the Lord, and we will honor his answer." Michael was gone.

Later after the meal, when the Valley seemed quiet, Daniel went to see Hagan, who was on top of the branches of the tree, staring out into the distance, stuck in his faraway place. Daniel decided to speak Enochian, which he rarely had attempted, "Excuse me, Hagan."

Hagan turned to look at him. "What is it, young Daniel?"

But Hagan already knew what Daniel was going to ask, for he had been expecting it for some time. "I would like to ask you a question, Hagan."

"Please ask," Hagan replied.

"I would like to know the reason why you cannot draw Breather of Life. Why must you have permission to draw your sword?" Hagan looked at Daniel and smiled. It was the first time Daniel could ever remember seeing Hagan smile. "I was expecting you to ask me that question, and I guess I do owe you the answer. It is the result of something that happened a long time ago and is the consequence of a great failure. I have not always looked as I look today. Now I am tall and slim with small wings and wear a long white robe. But there was a time when I was huge, almost as big as Michael, with wings that were large and powerful. I was full of strength, wearing battle armor made of gold. I was created by God to be the Warrior Defender." Daniel stared and listened. "But I did something I never should have done." Hagan took a deep breath and spoke the words he had never uttered to another angel. "I turned my back and rejected our Lord, the God of gods, the Lord of lords. I chose to follow another, one named Lucifer."

CHAPTER 7

Rapha, Saph, Lahmi, and Ishbi entered the gates of Jerusalem under a cloud of cover created by Asmodeus and fifty other demon angels swirling up the air into a light fog in the early evening. The demons would have loved to be able to lead the giants to the home of the King and deliver their message to him firsthand; however, access to King David was prevented by the host of soldiers in the physical world and the host of defenders in the spiritual world. King David, a man with a heart for God, was the central figure in Lucifer's plan to change the destiny of the world and to destroy God's salvation plan for His people. Destroy David and the prophecy could not be fulfilled. Destroy David and eliminate the arrival of the savior.

Lucifer, nor any other demon angel, was permitted to touch or harm God's people without permission from the Lord. They could harass, torment, tempt, and cause numerable anxiety but were not allowed to physically harm. The giants were different. Lucifer realized the great value that had been given him with the birth of Rapha. Rapha had been a mistake, yet Lucifer saw that this mistake could become his greatest weapon. Rapha was his killer.

It would be Rapha and his sons that would deliver the crushing blow to the Lord.

Abigail never recovered from the sadness of losing her Chileab. Although time had passed, it was a constant ache in her heart and her spirit that never dissipated. She would lie awake at night and wonder where he was, what he was doing, who was taking care of him. The unknown tormented her and caused her prayers to be filled with desperate pleas to the Lord to provide and care for Daniel. The worst pain came from the feeling of loneliness that engulfed her. Only David knew the truth about Daniel. Everyone in Jerusalem had assumed that Daniel died from illness, and sympathies had been dispersed to both the king and to Abigail.

Her only companion was Lizona, her handmaiden who was just around the same age as Daniel. In fact, Lizona and Daniel had grown up together, developing a remarkably close relationship. Lizona missed Daniel almost as much as Abigail. Together they would sit and share memories of Daniel that were special to each of them. Lizona would share how she loved to play jokes and to tease Daniel, how they would laugh at each other, how they loved to run off together and spy on the army soldiers as they took part in their training drills, how they would lie on top of the roof on warm summer nights, each trying to create animal figures out of the stars. Lizona shared how she loved to sing as Daniel played the harp, and how he always encouraged her to follow her dreams. Abigail would sit and listen, treasuring these memories inside her heart. Lizona would always say, "I know we are going to see him again, he will return." Abigail could only hope and pray that she was right.

She had not seen the king in over two years. Bathsheba was his newest wife and clearly had become his love. David did visit a few times soon after Daniel's departure, but he could never seem to find the words to comfort Abigail, and the visits would normally result in the king sitting and playing Daniel's harp with his eyes lifted to heaven. On his final visit, Abigail gave the harp to David and said, "This belongs to you now. I have no use for it. My only request would be that every time you play, you would cast prayers toward heaven for our son."

King David loved his many wives but found it hard to share the love among them all. Bathsheba was his eighth wife, and he was totally enamored with her, spending days and nights with her. She was beautiful and captivating; thus, it was only natural that David's other wives grew jealous. Abigail was not like that. She was jealous of no one and loved the king unconditionally. David knew deep in his heart that he should be spending more time with her and that Abigail deserved his love and attention, yet Bathsheba and her beauty...

The years passed. There would be no more marriages for Abigail, and she would bear no more children. She was the king's wife, a position filled with honor and respect, and every need she had was provided except the one item she needed the most, love. She had decided to petition David to allow her to leave Jerusalem and return home to Carmel to live among her people. Several years had passed since Chileab had been taken, and she felt the time was right for her to leave the city and return to the land of her birth. Abigail knew the king would most likely refuse her request as no wife was ever allowed to leave Jerusalem but decided she would risk the king's anger with hope that he would show her mercy and compassion. The letter of petition was written and ready to be delivered to the king.

In the foyer of her home, Abigail heard a commotion followed by the scream of Lizona. Outside the door lay the bodies of her household guards, four men known for their strength and protection. Abigail ran to the top of the stairway, looked down, and saw the giants.

The four giants were the most evil, wicked beings Abigail had ever laid eyes upon. Each was huge with armor and swords, beards dripping with spit and sweat. The leader looked up at her, and Lucifer whispered in his ear, "That is her, Abigail, wife of the king and mother to the boy."

Saph grabbed Lizona and was ripping her dress off her. "Rape her, but do not kill her. She is going to deliver a message for us," the demon whispered in his ear. Saph looked at his father who told him, "Take her with your brothers to the outer room. I will gather the woman."

Abigail was praying. There was nowhere to run and nowhere to hide as Rapha climbed the stairway; Lucifer, unseen by her, directly behind him. The stink from his breath was overwhelming as the giant moved closer, entering the chambers of Abigail. His hand reached for her throat when suddenly Rapha was thrown backward several steps. The archangel Michael had arrived and was standing directly in front of Abigail. Lucifer rose to his full height and stood in front of Michael, each staring at the other eye to eye. "Hello again, brother," said Lucifer.

The two most powerful angels within the spiritual world stood eye to eye, each with a hand on their mighty swords. Brothers. Created at the same time by the Lord of lords. One full of evil and wickedness and betrayal. One full of honor and holiness and truth. One the prince of the darkness. One the defender of the Lord. Each knew the battle must eventually be fought between them. Would it be here? Would it be now?

"Your plan will not succeed, brother," said Michael. "The coming of the savior has been foretold by the Lord, and He will arrive through the line of David, son of Jesse."

"So I have heard," replied Lucifer. "We shall see about that. I know that David's son who will continue the line has yet to be born."

"And how do you know that? Are you sure?" asked Michael.

"Do not play games with me, brother," said Lucifer. "Need I remind you that I am the Prince of this Earth, the Lord of the Darkness, the Keeper of Namok, and I know far more than you can imagine. I also know that you and I are destined for battle. Are you prepared to die today, Michael? You do not have the authority to stop me nor my giants from our work here. An archangel is no match for a lord."

"You are no lord, there is only one Lord and He is the God of gods, the maker of Heaven and Earth, El-Shaddai, Jehovah, and Ancient of Days. He alone will determine your fate and mine. You are correct, though, that I do not carry the authority to stop your giants this day, but I do bring you warning."

"You are so jealous of me, Michael. I can read it all over you. You and all the angels in the disgusting Valley of Eternity are simply regretting not being with me. You know how powerful I have become. You know the depth and width of my reach, the incomprehensible capacity I possess to direct and influence the behavior anyone, and, also, the ability to change the course of any event I choose. No, you are wrong, dear brother. I am the Lord. I am the true God. I am the Great Beast that can never be destroyed."

"Here is your warning, Lucifer. Should your giants harm the woman Abigail today, know that she will be with the Lord in Heaven and sing the praises and shout the glories and live eternally in heavenly peace. Know also that the boy will grow even stronger, and the events of today will not be kept from him. He will know, and he will avenge."

Lucifer spread his wings even wider, and his color turned to blood red. Smoke drifted from his nostrils, and fire came from his mouth. Evil permeated his presence. "I am Ruler of this World, the Serpent of Old, and the Risen Star. You will depart from me or you will die. Before you leave, please deliver a message for me." Lucifer drew his sword, Abaddon the Bringer of Death, held it high to the sky, and told Michael, "Tell Hagan he will die at my feet, Abaddon buried deep within him, and I will cut his wings and sever his head and toss his body to the four corners of the world." Michael stood tall and firm; he did not draw Tyrfing, but rather let Lucifer speak. "As for the boy Daniel, son of David, please tell him that he will choke on his own blood and see his own guts spill out onto the ground at the feet of my giants. I will allow Rapha to sever the boy's head, and the giants will drink his blood. David will fall. The line will be broken. The prophecy destroyed. My reign will continue forever! When I am ready, brother Michael, archangel from Heaven, you too will fall at my feet. It has been spoken."

Michael looked at Lucifer. He wanted to fight. Yet, he had not received the order of battle from God. His order for the moment was to deliver the message to Lucifer. And so he stepped aside as he watched Rapha approach sweet Abigail, mother of Daniel. Rapha grabbed her throat and brought her face close to his. The strength in Rapha's hand was not normal, thought Abigail, as she cried and prayed out to the Lord to save her. Rapha's eyes were dark and evil, his presence unlike any she had ever felt. He was not human; he was a monster, and she was powerless.

Rapha yelled for his sons to bring the girl, Lizona, up the stairway into the chamber of the king's wife. Saph, Lahmi, and Ishbi climbed the stairway, Lahmi carrying the girl on his shoulders. The chamber was full of demons, each hissing and shrieking because they saw the archangel standing in the corner, his hand still on the hilt of his sword. Demons continued to fill the room, hundreds and hundreds all clamoring to see what the giant would do. Lucifer whispered into the ear of Rapha, "It is time. Do what must be done."

"Please, please, please, don't," screamed Abigail. Rapha turned to Lahmi and told him to hold the girl upright so that she could see and give a full report to her king. Lizona was set down, head turned, forced to watch the giant Rapha as he turned back toward Abigail. "Tell your king what you have seen today!" shouted Rapha. "Tell him to gather his army, the Edomites are waiting to do battle, and we will fight with the Edomites. Tell him you have seen the giants, and we challenge him to find the courage to fight! We defy his kingdom, we defy his God, we spit on all that he stands for!"

"We have come to take everything from him. Today is just the beginning." Rapha worked his way behind Abigail so that Lizona could clearly see. He drew his small blade, grabbed Abigail's head, tilted it back, and quickly slit her throat. Lizona screamed from the depths of her soul. Blood was spurting everywhere, and the giants were laughing. Rapha placed his mouth upon the neck of Abigail and drank the blood that kept coming. When he finished, with blood running down his face and chest, he lifted his head to the sky and shouted, "For Lucifer! For Lucifer! For Lucifer!"

Michael stepped forward. The demons cowered away as he moved to the body of Abigail. A spirit emerged from her body, appearing almost as a ghost presence. Michael lifted the spirit and held it in his powerful arms. As he turned, he could hear the laughter coming from the demons. He knew he should not have, but he could not resist looking once more into the eyes of Lucifer. Michael said nothing; his eyes burned bright and golden. He would remember this day and would remember the laughter of his brother. Michael and the spirit of Abigail were gone.

Tears flowed from the eyes of the king as he listened to Lizona tell of the events. The giants had severed the head of Abigail and forced her to deliver it to his palace. David was filled with sadness but also regret. Regret that he had not treated Abigail better, had not spent more time with her, had not been there for her after the loss of Chileab. She had been a good woman, perhaps his wisest and most spiritual wife. Abigail had left her home and left her people to come to Jerusalem. She had never complained and had always fulfilled her duty. King David vowed in his heart that her death would be avenged. He needed to pray.

> *Why oh Lord, why did you allow this to happen?*
> *She was so innocent and so faithful,*
> *So full of love for her son.*
> *Where is her Chileab, where is Daniel?*
> *What is it you want me to do?*
> *Am I to fight against the armies of Edom?*
> *Am I to fight the giants from hell?*
> *Will you lift me up on the wings of eagles?*
> *And once again deliver me from the hands of my enemies?*

David would soon have his answer.

CHAPTER 8

"Lucifer was so sure of himself, so confident in his presence, so convincing that he was equal to God," Hagan was beginning his story to Daniel. "He was full of promises, and I was led astray. I took my focus off the Lord and off my purpose and cast my lot with Lucifer. I was not alone as I would estimate one-third of the angels in the valley chose to join the rebellion."

"The rebellion never really got started, though, as we were cast from the Valley of Eternity, banned from the heavenly realm, and thrown into an atmosphere above earth called Namok. We were free to roam and rule the earth, and that is what we did. We became the enemies of God, liars, persecutors, angels of darkness, adversaries of righteousness. I was there in the Garden of Eden when Lucifer became the father of lies, tempting the woman named Eve and bringing sin into the world. We were full of lawlessness and celebrated every victory over righteousness. Our thirst for evil grew, and we planted seeds of destruction into every mind possible. We were the tormentors of souls, seeking even the slightest invitation into the minds of the humans of earth. We were not permitted to physically harm the people, but we certainly were successful in stirring up evil in their spirits and leading them to harm and murder each other. And I was right there, participating in all of it."

Daniel could not believe what he was listening to. His trainer and mentor was actually a great deceiver and had been cast out of heaven. How was he here? How had he been allowed to return to the valley? David wanted to immediately ask those questions but sensed it may be best just to let the words and the story flow out of Hagan at his own pace and with his own timing.

"We were assigned regions of the earth. Our mission, like I said, was to create and promote any anti-God behavior. Again, God was our enemy, and we wanted the world to worship Lucifer, the prince of the Earth. My region included the Black Sea down through Ephesus to the southern tip of Egypt. I had thousands of demons under my command, and we were successful at creating hatred, misery, and the lust for evil. However, there was a small area south of the city of Tyre, west of Nazareth, located along the Mediterranean Sea called Haifa where a pocket of population existed who loved God and could not seem to be tempted to follow Lucifer. I began to take a personal interest in this region and spent more and more time there watching and listening and learning particularly from a family led by Boldak, a farmer with a wife and four daughters. I whispered into the ear of Boldak for many months, and the words I said to him are too shameful for me to even tell you, Daniel. We wanted to turn him from the Lord, for he was a respected leader in the community with many families under the sphere of his influence.

"Boldak had access to many seafarers, as they would dock in the port in Haifa and spend time while their ships were reloaded. Much of his success came from selling his crops to overseas markets. Boldak would share the story of God and his love and was beginning to convert more and more sea merchants who, in turn, would take the love of God to other areas. Lucifer became aware of Boldak and questioned me why this faith was growing in Haifa. I tried to explain my strategy of stirring up lust within the heart of the men surrounding the region, but he became irate with me and told me I must go to the hearts and minds of the daughters. Pick one and turn her, for that will pierce the heart of Boldak quicker than anything. I obeyed.

"For reasons I cannot remember, I chose the third daughter of Boldak as my target. Her name was Sedena, and she was beautiful. Aged around eighteen at the time, dark-haired, and full of life. She loved the Lord and spent much of her days in prayer. My challenge was to get into her spirit and her mind and begin to deposit seeds of rebellion, lust, anxiety, and fear. Her prayer life was so strong, and her faith and love of others was rooted so deep within her soul that I was unable to garner any success. Rather than growing frustrated about my failures, an unexpected feeling began to emerge within me. The feeling that I really wanted to have a conversation with this beautiful young girl.

"The only way for me to converse with Sedena was to metamorphize into the form of a human. There were only twelve of us who had the power to change to the form of a human being, and it was a risky thing to attempt because this power did not come from Lucifer but was given to us from the Lord when he created us. Lucifer urged us not to use this power because he could not guarantee we would be able to return to our original angelic form. But the more I was around Sedena, the more convinced I became that I had to risk it and establish dialogue with her. I did not realize it at the time, but Sedena was quietly ministering to my spirit and reviving a flame that had long been extinguished within me. Strange as this is for me to tell you, Daniel, I think I was falling in love with Sedena. Strange, because angels do not possess emotions like love. We are created by God for purpose, and I had been created to be a warrior defender. I think Lucifer sensed some sort of change in my spirit and warned me to begin the destruction of Boldak's family immediately. If I could not crush the spirit of Sedena, then I must move on to another daughter. He would intervene if needed.

"Daniel, I am telling you this because you will need to know this information in the future. God has brought you here for a reason and for a purpose. What I am about to tell you changed my path forever. I made the decision to metamorphize into the form of a young man traveling into the region of Haifa. My purpose was to establish a relationship with Sedena and have dialogue with her. She would end up teaching me much more than I would teach her."

King David stood when Nathan the prophet entered. "Greetings, Nathan. Thank you for coming. I will get directly to the point." Nathan already suspected what the king wanted to know, for the whole city continued to be in an uproar over the death of Abigail. Justice must be served. The giants must be destroyed, and the Edomites brought to their destruction. Surely, the king will call the forces, unify the army, and order the attack to avenge his wife. David had killed one giant in his youth; now was the time for more giant slaying. What King David did not know was the demon angels were out in full force in the city of Jerusalem, stirring up anger and hostility and the desire for revenge. The city grew angrier by the day, calling for the heads of the giants and the blood of the Edomites. Lucifer and his demons wanted David to lead his forces out against the Edomites. They would draw him in, trap the king, and the giants would once and for all destroy the prophecy of the line of David. The time had come.

The king was done with his mourning and was ready for battle. But he must be certain that God would give him victory and approve of his attack upon the Edomites. Therefore, the man of God, Nathan, had been summoned. Would God fight for his people? Did God wish for David to go to war with the Edomites and face the giants in battle?

"What does the Lord say?" asked David. "Is it his will for us to go to war? Will He bless the battle? Will he fight for us and give us victory?"

"I have been in deep prayer," answered Nathan, "and the Lord has given me specific instructions for you. You are to march and meet the Edomites in battle. You are to lead the forces yourself, and you are to do battle with the giant Rapha and his sons. I will give you a great victory and deliver my people from the hands of the Edomites. You are to go, and you are to lead the men, for I am with you and will not forsake you. Although these giants are much fiercer and far more brutal than the giant, Goliath, of your youth, nonetheless, nothing can stand against me. I am." Nathan finished by telling King David that this was the word he had received from the Lord.

David looked at Nathan. The king was truly a man after the Lord's own heart, and although he was far from perfect and had his own sinful nature, he tried to fully obey when the Lord gave a command. He trusted Nathan, for it was Nathan who had confronted him with his adultery over the sinful affair he had begun with Bathsheba. It was Nathan who had told David that it would not be he who would build a temple for the Lord, but rather his son and heir. And it was Nathan who was even now writing the history and recording the events of his reign up to this point. Although David had not worn the armor and led the forces in several years, as his mighty men and fiercest soldiers always insisted, he not be near the front lines, David would obey the word of the Lord from the prophet, Nathan. "Thank you, Nathan, may God continue to speak to you and through you."

Nathan left the home of the king, fully satisfied with his message and his delivery. As he walked the slight distance to his home near the eastern gate, he began to smile, and when he entered his home, he had regained his true form and his true presence. He was no longer Nathan the prophet but had reshaped back into Lucifer, the prince of the earth, and future Lord of all creation. Nathan had been poisoned and was near death. "Leave him lying there," Lucifer instructed Saph, who had accompanied him through the gap in the eastern gate. "If his God wishes to save him, let him save him. If he dies, then he dies."

As Lucifer and Saph stepped into the Jerusalem night, Lucifer turned and told Saph, "On second thought, go and slice your sword across the neck of Nathan the prophet, then cut out his heart and bring it to me. I will present it as a gift and a reward for your father, Rapha."

David issued the order to gather his forces. His armor was cleaned, and his sword sharpened. Joab, the commander of his forces, tried vehemently to talk the king out of leading the forces himself. "You are the king. You do not belong on the front lines. Let us fight for you and deliver a great victory into your hands. Your soldiers are ready to do whatever is necessary to defeat our enemies."

David refused to listen and instead simply stated, "I will lead. The Lord has spoken."

CHAPTER 9

Michael entered the gates of the Valley of Eternity riding the back of Pran, Uri following him in obedience. Normally, they would ride directly to the Tree of Trees, but this entrance would be different. They rode to the tree of Hagan and waited for Hagan and Daniel to emerge. As they emerged from the branches of the top of the tree, Michael spoke, "I have come from the presence of the Lord. Daniel, you have grown in strength and skill and are now ready to handle the sword of an angel. The Lord is pleased with you. You are to begin your sword training with Hagan. Our Lord has given me a sword, forged in the iron of Heaven and created by God himself. The sword is to be called Avigdor, which means defender and protector. With this sword, you will defend both humans on earth and angels in heaven. You will be the Great Defender."

Daniel did not know what to say. He simply stared at the archangel and watched as Michael asked Uri to hand him Avigdor. Daniel hardly noticed that the bells were ringing, and the thousands of angels had gathered in the air circling. The angels were singing a song, and although Daniel could not make out the full Enochian meaning of the song, he recognized the repeated phrase "sword of the Lord, sword of the Lord."

Michael drew Avigdor and held it up to the sky. It was the most magnificent sword Daniel had ever seen. It was huge and silver and had a yellow light that emanated from it. The hilt contained a silver cross-guard, and a tassel made of leather was attached to the pommel. The long blade had fuller slots along each flat side to lighten the weight of the blade. As Michael held it to the sky, all angels in the valley drew their swords and lifted them to heaven. It was sea of swords, a spectacular show of blades that covered the sky. The blades of heaven, the angelic swords welcoming a new member, Avigdor.

Michael's voice echoed across the valley. "There is one sword that is missing." Michael looked at Hagan. Hagan suspected what was about to be spoken, and if angels could cry, certainly his eyes would have been full of tears. He had not held his sword since the failure. He had been allowed to carry it all this time but could never draw it from its scabbard. It was a punishment for his crime and was an effective reminder of his rebellion. Though Hagan was remorseful and thankful for the Lord rescuing him from the Abyss, it was a warrior defender's worst punishment to carry a sword of swords, a sword of glory and be unable to wield it.

Michael continued, "Hagan, the Lord has listened to your request and has given permission for you to draw your sword, Breather of Life. He has removed the seal. Hagan, warrior-defender, you may draw your sword!"

Hagan stood up straight, lifted his wings to their full capacity, raised his head to the sky, and did the one thing he had dreamed about for such an exceedingly long time. He took his right hand, reached to the hilt, and drew the Breather of Life. The sword came alive immediately, and Hagan felt its power. The power of the defender sword crafted by the Lord. He held it to the sky, and it had the same yellow glow that emanated from Avigdor. Daniel could cry, and tears were flowing down his cheeks as he watched Hagan, his mentor, stand in strength with a presence of redemption filling his spirit. Thousands of angels also sensed the redemption of Hagan and began banging their swords together in a show of respect to both Hagan and his magnificent sword.

Michael handed Avigdor to Daniel who was amazed at the power and energy he felt from the blade. It felt as if it were part of him and was an extension of his arm, willing to do as it was commanded. Daniel had watched over time as other angels handled their swords, and he sensed that swords seemed to possess a lifelike personality. All swords were not equal, some being more powerful than others. There was a certain hierarchy among the angelic blades, and Daniel knew immediately that he was holding a blade near the top of that hierarchy. He raised it and held it side by side to Breather of Life. Two swords to fight for the Lord.

Tyrfing was lifted by Michael and held skyward, thus every sword in the Valley of Eternity was held to the highest heavens. These were the angels of heaven. Daniel felt for the first time that he was home.

Daniel and Hagan stood face-to-face in the training ground, each with their sword drawn and ready to practice battle technique movement. "I still want to hear more about your story, Hagan, about Sedena and your relationship with her and how you are here now in the valley."

"There will be time for more of my journey," Hagan replied. "But right now we must learn." The blade of Breather of Life suddenly pounded down upon the blade of Avigdor. Daniel could barely keep the sword in his hand as Hagan repeatedly attacked and retreated. It was attack and retreat, attack and retreat, over and over Hagan pounded Daniel and Avigdor until Daniel eventually dropped his blade and lie on his back staring up at the point of Breather of Life.

"You are not controlling your spirit! You have forgotten all the movements we have practiced over and over! Your mind and your body and your spirit are all acting independently! Your total focus is on your sword! That is not the path to victory!"

Daniel would always rise, and in what seemed like a mere moment, he was back upon the ground. Hagan was relentless and would show no mercy. His quickness was beyond belief, and his swordsmanship was mesmerizing. Breather of Life was alive and seemed hungry for battle. The sword became more intense the longer Hagan wielded it. Daniel could feel Avigdor wanting more, wanting to attack, wanting to meet the challenge, but he could not give his blade what it wanted. It was almost as if Avigdor was calling to Daniel, "Come on, boy, let my power be unleashed!"

Hagan hit Daniel with the side of his blade, knocking him down yet again. "You are off balance, why are you not flying?" As Daniel lay finally exhausted and unable to move, he let go of Avigdor, letting the blade rest by his side. Hagan took the tip of Breather of Life, placed it next to the cheek of Daniel and ever so slightly cut down through the cheek, blood dripping down Daniel's face. "Let that scar be a reminder of this day." Hagan took his left hand, held it out, and spoke to Avigdor, "Come to me." Avigdor immediately flew into the hand of Hagan who now held both swords. "You have made a fatal mistake that you should never make again." Hagan stood over Daniel. "Never relinquish your sword! It is part of you, let it become part of you. Your blade will fight for you, let its power be released. You do not control Avigdor, nor does Avigdor control you. You are equals and must become one in spirit. You must control your spirit and your movement. Focus on the blade of your opponent. What does it like, how does it move, is there any weakness?"

Hagan handed Avigdor back to Daniel who was now sitting. "Get up. Let us gather some nourishment before we battle again. I also want to tell you some more about Sedena."

After the meal, Hagan began again, "I was a young man, going by the name Hadrach, traveling to the ports of Haifa so that I could gain employment on one of the trading ships. My story was that I wanted to see the world. I stopped on the farm of Boldak and was quickly shown the love of God as he invited me into his home for a meal. I sat among his family and listened as they talked of the Lord and his goodness and mercy. Of course, I was intentional in striking up conversation with Sedena. My one meal turned into many as I was offered employment as a farmhand. I told Boldak that I would work for several months, save up some money and then gain employment on one of the trading ships.

"My mission was the destruction of Boldak through the manipulation of Sedena, yet I found it increasingly difficult to plant my seeds of deception and corruption. Sedena and I grew closer and closer. Every time I would mention my disbelief in God and that I felt humans should be able to live their lives any way they wanted, doing whatever pleased them, Sedena would immediately say, 'That is not what I believe.' She would go into a long discourse on the laws of God.

"I tried to lure her to accept the fact that there were other gods equal to her god. I talked to her about Ashtoreth, the goddess of fertility, and Baal, the god of the Canaanites, who allowed the earth to bear crops. There was Chemosh, the national god of the Moabites who offered immense blessings as a result of human sacrifice. And Dagon, the god of water and grain with the body of a fish and a human head worshipped by the Philistines. I told her of Lucifer and his goodness and the fact that my family worshipped him and told of his birthright and his kingdom in Namok. I asked if she would be willing to learn more about Lucifer and perhaps even offer a prayer to him. She would just stare at me, listening patiently until I was finished, then reply, 'My God is the Ancient of Days, the God of Noah and of Moses, and of Joshua. The people of my God are the Israelites, yet he offers his love to everyone.' She would always turn it back and personally minister and witness to me. I think she was beginning to think of me as more than just a friend but needed me to accept her God and accept her beliefs.

"Our friendship grew, and I did indeed begin to listen to her teachings. I began to dwell again on the Valley of Eternity and the holiness of the Lord. Her faith and her purity moved me. The mistake that had been made consumed me, and I knew that there was no pathway home. I had made my decision. Yet, I continued to listen and be drawn into this family of true believers. We shared our first kiss on a picnic next to a small pond that bordered their main field. She told me she was falling in love with me, and I began to realize I could never do anything to harm this sweet girl. I loved her."

Hagan stopped and looked at Daniel. "I know this sounds hard to believe, but I assure you, young Daniel, it happened exactly as I am saying. I began to get scared because I did not know what I was going to do. I wanted to stay with Boldak and Sedena and the rest of the family. I wanted to commit to following God, and I never wanted to become Hagan, warrior-defender turned Lucifer follower again. To return to my old ways of deceiving and blinding the minds of people so that they cannot see the truth began to seem unfathomable. Under no circumstances did I want to return to the promotion of false doctrine. No longer did I desire to torment followers of God, nor persuade people to do evil acts. I just wanted to live as Hadrach.

"How long could I live in the form of Hadrach? Would I be released from my demon responsibilities? Will God allow me to become his follower as Hadrach? Will God forgive me? What is Lucifer going to say? What will become of Breather of Life? Should I tell Sedena the truth? All of these were questions that were pounding through my consciousness.

"I met with Boldak and told him of my love for his daughter, told him I wanted to marry her and make her the happiest girl in the world. Told him of my commitment to the Lord and my repentance of unbelief. I told this great follower of God that I had committed many sins and had traveled many dark paths in my lifetime, but that I was sorry and wanted to live with the love of God in my heart. I wanted to follow the law of God from this point forward. Everything I told him was the absolute truth. However, obviously, I failed to tell him I had really been created as an angel in heaven and turned my back on the Lord Almighty choosing instead to follow the Great Deceiver." Hagan chuckled, and Daniel even had to smile a little when he heard that. "Yeah, I guess that would have been a little hard for him to believe."

Daniel replied. "What did Boldak say to you?"

"Boldak looked me directly in my eyes and said words to me that touched me to my core. He said, 'Who am I to deny my daughter the love of her life? Though I sense trouble and turmoil within your spirit, I also sense a rising goodness that is trying to overtake the darkness. I can only pray to my God to allow His Light to defeat the enemy's darkness. I know not much of where you come from, what you have been, deeds you have done, but my trust and my faith in the Lord allow me to believe He has brought you to us, and He has brought you into the life of my Sedena. Yes, Hadrach, you have my blessing'.

"I asked Sedena to be my wife under a full moon on a warm summer's evening. She fell into my arms shouting, 'Oh, Hadrach, oh, Hadrach, yes, a thousand times, yes!' For the first time since the rebellion, I felt peace in my spirit. No longer was I Hagan, defender of Lucifer, commander of demons, sower of destruction. I had become Hadrach, lover of God, searcher for truth, husband of Sedena."

All was well under that full moon. And then Lucifer appeared.

"That is enough for now," said Hagan. "Come, we must train."

Left, right, up, down, Hagan swung the great sword time and again at Daniel. This session was not about attacking and retreating but, rather, was all about attacking. Again, Hagan was relentless, never allowing Daniel to gain any momentum. Daniel was not falling continuously but could not land any significant strikes with Avigdor. Hagan was spinning and striking, and Daniel began to get a sense of the greatness of Hagan. He was impossible to counter, his quickness too much for Daniel. When Hagan finally halted his attack, Daniel's head was spinning. He looked down and saw the valley floor far beneath him, never realizing during the battle that he had been flying.

"You have made progress," Hagan proclaimed. "I hit you with blow after blow, and you were able to counter most of them, but most importantly, you stayed flying and moving with me through the air. That tells me your mind and your body were totally focused on what is possible rather than what is not possible. For you to become the Great Defender, you must never allow your spirit to dwell on restrictions and limitations, but you must instead believe in what is unbelievable. Trust and believe in the power of God, for the battle is ultimately His anyway. You should never fight with any fear. Respect your opponent? Absolutely. But always remember that you fight for a power that is undefeatable. You fight for a power that knows no bounds. Jehovah-Jireh."

Time passed. Training continued. Daniel improved. Avigdor began to trust Daniel, and Daniel began to trust Avigdor. Together they sparred and learned. Avigdor wanted to be turned loose, to be released to deliver crushing blow after crushing blow, but Daniel was not quite ready to totally let the blade strike free.

Then it happened. Mahlon, Bildad, and Daniel were fighting each other on the training ground. Hagan insisted Daniel learn technique against multiple opponents, instructing Mahlon and Bildad to go hard and beat down Daniel as much as possible. Daniel was focused, controlling his spirit, perfect balance between his body and mind. Bildad lifted into the air, spinning around to Daniel's right side while Mahlon attacked the left. Mahlon delivered a thrust designed to knock Daniel off balance. Everything seemed slow to Daniel, and he saw it coming, lifting his body into the air, avoiding the strike from Mahlon while Avigdor delivered a devastating blow to the sword of Bildad. Bildad lost his grip as his sword fell to the ground beneath him. Avigdor at the throat. "I yield," murmured Bildad. Daniel felt Mahlon behind him ducked and spun to his right, turning to face the sword of the angel he had long admired as the best in the defender realm.

Mahlon attacked. Avigdor took each blow and cast it aside. The two were flying in the air causing quite a scene as both took turns attacking. Daniel was feeling and seeing everything so clearly, almost anticipating each blow from Mahlon. The battle continued, and Daniel could feel Avigdor growing more powerful, he and Daniel in unison, moving and acting as one. Mahlon was good, and he too felt power surging through his angelic spirit.

Hagan was watching every move. He already knew what the outcome would be and was not surprised when it finally happened.

The sword of Mahlon felt an advantage, hammering down upon Avigdor, going for the victory. Daniel retreated, taking each blow with a step backward. Mahlon flipped into the air, landing quickly behind Daniel and delivered a slice into Daniel's shoulder. It was not a serious thrust, yet it cut the skin, and blood began to drip from the shoulder. As Daniel looked at the cut, Mahlon swung his blade at the legs, causing Daniel to stumble and fall. On the ground, Daniel turned and looked into the eyes of Mahlon; he was expected to yield, but instead, leapt up, let out a cry, and lifted Avigdor, allowing his blade to finally be free. Avigdor was hungry and powerful, and Daniel swung with strength and grace. Blow after blow caused Mahlon to retreat. Angels all around watching, recognizing the beauty and power of Daniel and Avigdor.

Mahlon was on his back, Avigdor placed directly at his throat. The battle joy was in the spirit of Daniel, and his eyes were wide. Mahlon was speaking, "I yield. I yield." Daniel did not even hear, his blade pressing further into the neck of Mahlon. Breather of Life hammered onto the side of Avigdor with a sound that could be heard throughout the Valley of Eternity. Daniel and his blade went sprawling to the side, Mahlon staggering to his feet. Hagan looked at Daniel with a look of anger, "Your opponent yielded. Do you not accept his submission?" Hagan continued, "It is your choice to accept or not. Just know if you do not accept, you will battle myself and the Breather right now."

Daniel was back on his feet, looking and listening to Hagan "I did not hear the yield. I do not wish to battle you, Hagan. Yes, I accept." Daniel turned to Mahlon. "I am sorry, my friend, I lost focus." Mahlon nodded, accepting the words and was gone.

Hagan placed Breather of Life back into its scabbard, walked toward Daniel, and spoke, "Young Daniel, you have grown powerful and possess a magnificent blade. You are making progress, but you must always remember it is up to you to control your power and use it only for good. The battle joy will come, but it must not overtake your spirit, and it must not overtake your mind. Never allow Avigdor to do something that you do not want him to do."

Daniel understood. "Yes, thank you, Hagan. I have learned much this day."

CHAPTER 10

Baal-Achbor was the king of the Edomites. Located south of Jerusalem, the Edomites were a proud people who had been defeated by David and his army eight years earlier. Forced to become a vassal of Israel, Edom was fertile ground for Lucifer and his demons. Much effort had gone into sowing seeds of rebellion and hatred toward King David. Asmodeus had commanded the effort of penetrating the minds and spirits of the Edomites. Evil rituals had grown, sacrifices had become common, and worship of the god, Baal, had skyrocketed. Lust, greed, and jealousy were rampant. Morality was all but forgotten, and the people of Edom took anything their hearts desired.

Asmodeus had been constantly speaking into the spirit of Baal-Achbor until, at last, the rebellion was ready to proceed. "You have done nice work with the soul and mind of Baal-Achbor," Lucifer told Asmodeus. "He seems ready to lead his army north to draw out King David. It is time for him to meet Rapha."

The Edomite army was gathered and ready to begin the march, one hundred thousand strong. The king was sitting in his tent, ready to begin the campaign next morning. Lucifer entered, unseen by Baal-Achbor, his evil presence ready to be invoked. The chief of arms entered the tent and told the king, "There is a visitor here to see you, my king. He is giant of a man who says he comes in friendship."

"Let him in," whispered Lucifer into the ear of Baal-Achbor.

"My name is Rapha, from the region of Haifa, loyal follower of Lucifer. I am the great giant, the killer of thousands, the warrior of warriors. I have three sons who fight by my side, and we cannot be defeated. I have come to kill for you, King Baal-Achbor."

"I have heard of you and your sons, Rapha the giant. Your reputation is far and wide. You are welcome amidst my army."

"I have several stipulations before we commit to your service," Rapha responded. "First, my sons and I are not assigned to any unit. We fight where and when we choose. We take orders from no one." He continued, "Second, I will be the one to kill King David, with no mercy shown. Third, you will no longer worship Baal but will bow at the feet of Lucifer, the Lord of Darkness, the prince of the earth, the king of Namok. These three stipulations are non-negotiable." Rapha stared at Baal-Achbor, waiting for his response. Asmodeus whispered, "If he does not agree, slit his throat, rip his heart."

"Stipulation one and stipulation two are agreed upon. However, I do not know your Lucifer. I worship Baal, the ancient of gods, the lord of nature, and the bringer of victory."

"I have spoken," Rapha said. "I have said these are non-negotiable. Lucifer will have his victory over David. Your army will fight the Israelites with or without you."

Baal-Achbor knew he was in tough situation. This Rapha was not someone to oppose. Lucifer decided to intervene and reveal his true presence to the king of the Edomites. Lucifer appeared in his true form. Wings spread, arms out, red robe underneath golden armor. His hair was silver, and his skin light red. He did not have just one set of wings but had three sets, each made of black oily feathers. A red glow shone around his entire presence. The sword of Lucifer, Abaddon, was hidden beneath his robes.

Baal-Achbor could not believe what he was seeing. Frozen, unable to move or speak, he just stared. It was the most beautiful and the most horrific creature he could imagine. Power unlike any he had ever felt, he had no choice but to bow to his knees falling prostrate upon the ground. "You are my Lord" were the only words that would come out of his mouth.

Lucifer said nothing. As Baal-Achbor lifted his head slightly to gaze once again, the head of Lucifer became the head of a dragon, with eyes of fire and smoke exiting the nostrils. The mouth of the dragon opened, and the king felt for sure he would be consumed. Suddenly, Lucifer was gone. Nothing but silence for many minutes, Baal-Achbor remained prostrate, still unable to move. Rapha spoke, "You have seen the Lord! You have bowed! We will defeat the Israelites, and I will cut out the heart of King David to feed the dragon. Nothing can stand before us! We march north in the morning!" Rapha exited the tent.

Baal-Achbor eventually rose and knew he would soon be king over Edom, Israel, and Judah.

Daniel's training sessions with Hagan had become must-watch activities among the angels in the Valley of Eternity. Thousands would hover over the session, watching as Hagan, the master warrior-defender, would spar and teach the young human-angel, Daniel. Hagan taught Daniel every move he could imagine, taught him how to read an opponent's sword, how to control his spirit, how to balance his mind and body. Perhaps most importantly, he taught Daniel how to become one with Avigdor. "It is a fine balance, the relationship between defender and sword. You must allow it freedom to feed its hunger for battle, yet it must know you are master. Avigdor was created by the Lord and is your gift to serve as your partner in the battles that are to come," Hagan spoke as he and Daniel sat among the branches high in the tree after finishing a thorough day of training.

"Why do you keep speaking of the battles to come?" asked Daniel. "Who am I going to fight? Am I going to fight Lucifer?"

"I do not know the Lord's will. I have my suspicions, but the Lord is Lord. What I do know is you were brought here for a reason. We all have purpose. We were created for purpose and must be prepared when that purpose needs fulfilling. I do sense a coming battle, and I want you to be prepared to be the defender you were meant to be."

Daniel sat quietly. Hagan sat quietly. "Will you fight by my side when I am called to battle?" Daniel finally asked.

Hagan did not respond for a long time. "That I do not know, young one."

"You have never finished your story about Sedena. You only mentioned that Lucifer came to see you right before you were to marry. What happened, Hagan? Can you tell me?"

Again, Hagan sat quietly. For a long time, he said nothing, staring out across the Valley of Eternity. Daniel thought he was in some kind of trance and eventually decided he should leave. As he was getting up, Hagan finally broke his silence. "I am ready to share more of my story, Daniel. Lucifer appeared to me on the night under the full moon after I asked Sedena to become my wife. I made up some vague excuse to her and told her I must attend to some business, escorting her home. She was so happy as we said good night. 'I will see you tomorrow, Hadrach, we have so much to plan. I love you.' 'I love you too,' I responded with Lucifer hovering over my shoulder.

"'Well, isn't that lovely?' Lucifer spoke as we made our way to my quarters. 'I send you to destroy this family and now you are trying to join it, Hagan, or should I say Hadrach? This is unacceptable. You will return to your true form, never to return to this place. I will send a replacement to wreck this family and destroy the faith of Boldak as well as this silly little girl, Sedena. You have failed me, Hagan.' I looked at Lucifer, the prince of darkness, and knew what I must say. 'Lucifer, I am Hagan, the warrior-defender, and I know the path I chose when I followed you during the rebellion. We turned against the Lord and were cast from heaven to Namok and eventually to earth. We have been allowed to roam the earth doing the work of evil, and I have always fulfilled my responsibilities. Until now. I can no longer serve you. I am no longer Hagan. I do not know how long I can remain in this form, but for however long I am allowed, I am going to live as Hadrach. I am going to marry Sedena, and we are going to worship the one true God.

"'You cannot physically harm me, Lucifer. For it is impermissible for any demon-angel to harm followers of God. I am a follower of God. I invoke his protection.' Lucifer let out a roar that could be heard all the way to Namok. Rising to his full strength, he allowed his full evilness to be seen. I must admit, Daniel, even I, the powerful and forceful warrior-defender, was shaken by his fury. I had never seen Lucifer, who was created and began his life as the Morning Star, lose self-control in such a way. He looked down at me, head of a dragon, eyes of red, breathing sparks of fire and spoke these words. 'You are dead to me, Hagan. You will regret this life you have chosen. You will not be Hadrach forever, and when you are finished with this charade, you will feel my wrath and know the power of the prince of the earth.' And then he reverted to his normal face, looked at me with piercing eyes and ever so calmly said, 'Remember this. Any offspring you produce with this silly girl will be half-human and half-angel and will not be exempt from my harm and my power. Enjoy your little marriage, Hagan, but be careful not to produce any offspring.'

Lucifer laughed and said, 'I have a feeling we will see each other again very soon, Hadrach.' He was gone."

Hagan turned to Daniel and said, "Talk about being in a tough situation. Here I was with a beautiful new wife and a part of an amazing God-fearing family, and I knew if Sedena ever got pregnant, Lucifer would be right back in our lives."

"Did Sedena want children?" asked Daniel.

"Are you kidding?" said Hagan. "Almost immediately, she began making plans for a baby. Unless I was incapable of producing a child, I knew it was going to be impossible to prevent her from getting pregnant. I tried not to think about it and to enjoy each moment we had together. To live in the moment became my goal because of course I never really knew how much time I had as Hadrach. I knew I had the power to metamorphize, but God could have taken away my human form at any moment. I prayed, I lived, I loved, moment by moment, day by day.

"Time passed. We were happy. I was beginning to take more responsibility on the farm as Boldak was spending much of his time on the docks speaking to the seafarers about God. He would bring some of them to the farm, and we would eat and hear about faraway places. Sedena would always get a wistful look in her eyes, for she really wanted to travel and see the world and go to unknown places. She had an adventurous spirit that needed to fly.

"A particular traveler named Demetrius visited the farm one day and was telling us all about his travels, specifically describing an island named Cyprus, full of beautiful gardens and immaculate climate. The people were friendly and welcoming to all. I knew Sedena was itching to travel. There was something, though, I did not like about this Demetrius. He seemed to avoid eye contact with me but was focusing entirely on Sedena, who was captivated by the stories of his travels.

"Demetrius offered to allow us passage on his ship to travel to Cyprus and see the beauty firsthand. I began to question him about his business, his ships, and very briefly made direct eye contact. What I saw caused the hair on the back of my neck to stand. For in those eyes and behind the charm and engaging personality, I saw…" Hagan had suddenly stopped talking. It was as if he was there in Haifa with

Sedena. Daniel sat without speaking as well. He knew something or some feeling was marinating within the spirit of Hagan. His eyes went to the sky, and if angels could cry, Hagan's eyes would surely have been full of tears. He began again, "It was at that exact moment I knew I would never be able to have a normal life with Sedena. There would be no escaping who I truly was. I was the warrior-defender who had rejected the Lord of Lords. I would forever be linked with Lucifer and his demons. How had I ever thought I could escape and begin again? For as I looked into the eyes of Demetrius, I saw the eyes of Asmodeus.

"He knew, and he just smiled. I stood up and rudely told Demetrius to leave and not come back. He was not welcome. Sedena tried to intervene. She could not believe I had suddenly become so inhospitable to such a polite guest. 'Please stay,' she kept saying to Demetrius. 'I want to hear more of Cyprus.' But I insisted. Demetrius agreed it would be best to leave and apologized if he had said or done something that had offended me. Before he turned to exit, he bowed to Sedena and told her he hoped they would see each other again. Once more, he looked at me. My hand could not help but go to where Breather of Life normally sat. If I had been wearing my sword, I would have killed. Sedena was furious with me. That night, we had our first real fight. She kept saying it seemed as if I was keeping something from her. I had to tell her. She deserved to know the truth."

"You decided to tell her everything?" Daniel asked.

"Everything," Hagan said. "I told her my story from the beginning. My creation in the Valley of Eternity. My purpose as the warrior-defender. My decision to follow Lucifer, the Morning Star, and how we were kicked out of heaven under the sound of thunder and crashing of lightning. I told her of Breather of Life and my role to bring calamity and destruction upon the earth. I told her about my mission to destroy her family and her faith. Her love had changed everything. Changed my heart, my mind, my purpose. I told her how much I loved her and that I did not know how much time I had as Hadrach. Finally, I told her I had seen the eyes of Asmodeus."

"Did she have trouble believing?" Daniel asked.

"Well, she really didn't have too long to sit and think about it since we found ourselves in each other's arms, full of passion. I just wanted her to know how much she meant to me and how much she had changed me and how much I loved her. We hugged and kissed, and the passion was something I had never felt before. Sedena and I made love that night over and over. That was the night, Daniel, Sedena became pregnant with our child.

"She was so happy to be pregnant, and though we spoke more about my past and she asked me many questions, particularly about why I had turned my back on God, her main focus seemed to be on the pregnancy and preparing to bring a child into this world. She loved me, and I loved her, and together we would love our child. I knew though things were about to change. Remember what I told you Lucifer had said about our offspring? He had threatened any child of mine, saying it would be half-human, half-angel and declared he had the ability and the right to intervene in its life. I knew Lucifer well enough to know he did not make idle threats. Where could we hide? Was there somewhere we could go to protect our child? How could we hide from the prince of the earth?

"I prayed and prayed and asked God to protect Sedena and the child. Daniel, if I am being honest, I must admit I do not know if God heard me, and I said no prayers for myself. I also did not talk to Sedena about the child being half-human, half-angel as I thought that would just upset her. I also lied to you, Daniel, when I said I told her everything. I did not tell her about Lucifer's threat to any children we would have. Certainly, her world had already been rocked. After all, she had been told she was married to an angel in disguise and that everything she believed about her husband had been a lie. I just could not force myself to tell her Satan himself would be coming for her child.

"Deep down, I knew what was going to happen, knew that in a few months, the world I had grown to love and the family that had loved me in return would be taken from me. There was no sense in trying to run, nowhere we could go and nowhere we could hide. Plus, Sedena would need to be around her family when the inevitable occurred. She insisted the child inside her was a son, and who was I to argue with the maternal instincts of a woman? For me, son or daughter, it did not matter because of the instinct of dread I had within my spirit. I just tried to enjoy each day and to again live in the moment. But it was impossible, Daniel. Impossible because I knew Lucifer was coming for my son, and I knew that I was about to fight the legions of Namok for everything I loved.

"Just a few weeks before the delivery, on a foggy, chilly morning, Sedena woke early and shook me. 'I have it, Hadrach. I know the name for our son. It came to me, and I want to share it with you.' I asked her to please tell me. What would be the name of our son? She said his name would mean 'God heals.' Telling me that God had healed me from a life of sin and rebellion. God was a healer and miracle worker and had a mighty purpose for me. She looked at me and said our son would be named Rapha."

CHAPTER 11

"Gadir was a merchant on the docks of Haifa I had become friends with. He was not wealthy and had only a small vessel sailing to places nearby and trading just enough to survive. But I trusted him. As the birth was imminent, I met with him, told him not to ask any questions, gave him more gold than he had ever seen before. I told him to be ready if something out of the ordinary happened on our farm. The instructions I gave was to get Sedena, and child if possible, and take her somewhere, anywhere, far away from this place and make sure she was cared for and protected and had everything she needed. Gadir was puzzled at my request, but I simply said, 'You may not understand now, but the day is fast approaching when you will. I am counting on and trusting in you Gadir.'

"It was early in the morning when Rapha came. I went to get the nurse maid who would help with the delivery, but before leaving, I gave Sedena a kiss and told her how much I loved her and thanked her for healing me. I said I would love her forever. She grabbed my hand and said she loved me and that she could not wait for me to see my son. I kissed her one more time and was out the door.

"Daniel, those were the last words I ever spoke to Sedena.

"I stood outside the door as the nurse maid and Sedena's sisters went about the delivery process. I could hear Sedena screaming and calling my name. But that was not the only sound I heard, Daniel. I also heard a mob coming down the street toward the farm. I looked hard and finally saw a group of about thirty men as they appeared on the horizon, probably half a mile away. Boldak heard them as well and gathered an old sword and a long bamboo-stick he kept hidden away.

"We had seven men who worked with us on the farm, and they came running as well, carrying whatever tool they had. The leader of the mob was Demetrius. I knew instantly that demons were everywhere, inciting these men and filling these men with rage and madness and furor. Each was armed and coming to kill, rob, and destroy. As they drew closer, I had a decision to make. I could fight as Hadrach and kill as many of the men as possible. Or I could reshape back into Hagan and fight the demons."

Hagan turned to Daniel and asked him, "What would you have done had you been in the same situation?"

Daniel thought for a moment and decided, "I think I would have returned to my true identity and drawn the Breather of Life to destroy the demons. You said you were huge and powerful. I would have let that power be unleashed."

"Well, that is the choice I made. I metamorphized back into Hagan, the warrior-defender, and drew Breather of Life ready to fight the horde of demons, many whom I had once led. Asmodeus immediately withdrew from Demetrius and rose to meet me in the air. He was surrounded by hundreds of demons all hissing and closing in on me. 'You betrayed us, Hagan,' Asmodeus said. 'Now you must accept your fate and pay the price.' We fought. Asmodeus is a very powerful demon. He fights with two swords, Death and Hell, and both blades are formidable. But if you are to ever fight him, Daniel, I want to give you one piece of advice. Always place your central focus on the sword called Hell, for Hell always follows Death. He will switch hands with the swords but will never swing Hell before he swings Death."

"I assume you did not kill Asmodeus?" asked Daniel.

"No. We fought, but my power felt slightly off for some reason. It was probably because my mind was on Sedena and the birth and Boldak trying to fend off the mob. I was also not only fighting Asmodeus but also a horde of demons surrounding me. Breather of Life was doing its job, keeping me alive, but I could not gain an advantage. There were just too many."

"I do not understand, Hagan. Where were the defenders? Where was the army of angels from the valley? Where was Michael?"

"Oh, they were there, Daniel. We were surrounded by thousands of defender angels. But they could not come to my aid. Remember, I was the enemy. I had been cast out of heaven. I had betrayed God and turned my back on the defender realm. Mahlon was there, Bildad, Gad, all the defenders you have become a part of, but they could not help. The laws of God would not allow it."

"Then why were they there? Why did they surround you?"

"They were there not for me, but for Boldak, his family, and, of course for Sedena. After a particularly intense sequence of fighting with Asmodeus and the horde, I retreated to the room where Sedena was giving birth. Asmodeus did not pursue, using this time instead to reorganize his demons, for I had taken the life and heads of many. As I entered the room, I saw the most amazing vision. I saw my son being born. Sedena was pushing and screaming as the nurse maid said, 'He is almost here.' And just like that, Rapha was in this world. Half-human, half angel, the nurse maid held him in her arms and then lifted him up to the sky. Then all hell broke loose.

"I remember the nurse maid holding Rapha, then suddenly she was not the nurse maid anymore but was Lucifer, the prince of darkness, holding my son. Lucifer quickly flew out of the room, carrying Rapha with him. I looked at Sedena, who strangely was still pushing and caught a glimpse of another child, a daughter coming into the world. Twins! Sedena's sister had stepped in and was holding this baby girl in her arms. Sedena was screaming hysterically, 'Our son! Our son! Hadrach!' I flew after Lucifer. Lucifer had handed Rapha to Asmodeus, who, surrounded by demons, was gone. I took chase, but there was no way I could catch them. My son was gone. My spirit, my being, my entire existence was shattered. I was destroyed and defeated and simply did not care anymore. I flew straight toward Lucifer.

"Lucifer must have realized or felt something important was going on with Sedena because he was heading directly back to her as I chased. But right as he was about to enter the room and steal away the baby girl, a flash of light emanated, and a huge wall was created around the farm. A wall of light. A wall of angels. A wall of defenders. And Michael was there. My wife, Boldak, and his entire family were under the protection of the Defender Realm. Lucifer pulled up, directly in front of Michael, who had drawn Tyrfing, ready to fight under the name of the Lord. The thing, Daniel, you must understand about Lucifer is he does not like to fight when the odds are not in his favor. For all his evil and all his wickedness, he knows, deep down in his innermost being, he cannot defeat the Lord and cannot stand in the presence of the light of God. And so he plots and devises his schemes and evil plans under the canopy of darkness, always looking for an advantage. He had no advantage here, as Michael was not going to allow him any further access to the family of Boldak.

"And just as he was about to speak to Michael, I hit Lucifer as hard as I could in the back, sending him flying. Lucifer turned and had Abaddon ready to fight the Breather of Life. I was reckless. The battle madness had overcome me, and I swung with all my force time and again. I was fighting with hatred and for the revenge of the life that had been taken from me. For my son, Rapha, who had been stolen from me, and for Sedena, whom I would never see again. I was fighting evil itself, Lucifer, the Satan of the world. His three sets of wings were flying in full power and his head, again, had become the head of a dragon. His sword had also become fire, and though I matched him move for move and chased him in the air, I began to feel his true evil and sensed that he was just drawing me into him.

"Daniel, I was powerful, and I knew how to fight, and I battled him for a long time. Striking him with every move possible, attacking and withdrawing, looking for the right time to deliver the death blow from the Breather of Life. Michael stood and watched, never leaving the wall of light. Boldak escorted his family out the back of the home, carrying Sedena and the baby toward the docks. The wall of light surrounding them moved as they moved. If I felt any solace, it was that at the very least, I was distracting Lucifer from Boldak and his family. Demons began to gather around Lucifer, and I began to understand the battle was not going to end well."

Daniel had to ask what he was thinking. "Why wouldn't Michael and the angels help you, Hagan? You had changed and left behind your evil ways. They should have fought alongside you."

"Remember what I have taught you about angels," Hagan said. "We are creatures created for a purpose, and we serve the Lord and perform His tasks. Michael and the angels were there to protect Boldak, Sedena, and the others. They were not there to fight my battle. To them, I was still a rebel who had been cast out of heaven. This was not their fight. They performed their mission as they protected the family, leading them to Gadir and his waiting ship. The light stayed at the docks for a long time. Gadir took my family away. I do not know where they went or what became of them. I only knew the light stayed at the docks because I saw it as Lucifer was pounding me over and over. Abaddon had finally knocked the Breather of Life from my hands as demons were behind me hitting and stabbing. I could not battle Lucifer and the demons at the same time. He was just too powerful. As my sword flew from my hand, Lucifer began taunting me, 'You are nothing, Hagan. You are worthless. I told you that you would regret choosing to worship God. Where is your God now? Is he coming to your rescue? Where is Michael?'

"I sank to my knees in the air as demons held my arms. Blow after blow. I was losing consciousness. I knew he would sever my head any moment. The end was near. Demons were cutting my wings in half. With each blow from the prince of darkness, I was being reduced in size. My strength was gone, my wings were cut, my great size disappeared. No longer was I the mighty defender. Satan was chopping me down. Lucifer grabbed me by my hair, tilted my head back, and breathed evil smoke into my face. His dragon tongue licked me before he morphed back into his normal head. 'Killing you would be too easy, Hagan. How dare you challenge my authority. I am going to cast you into the Abyss where you will dwell forever. You will be paralyzed, floating in darkness, wanting to speak and move but never again will you be heard from. You will be trapped inside a coffin, buried alive, rotting away like the piece of filth that you are. And as you float inside the Abyss, know that I will be a father to your son, Rapha. I will raise him in wickedness, and he will know nothing but evil. I will teach him to kill, torment, and destroy. He will be my giant, my killer, and I will use him to destroy the will of God. Goodbye, Hagan.'

"With those words, he picked me up by the hair, spun me around, and threw me into the Abyss. I was finished. I was surrounded by darkness, paralyzed, alone. It was pure torment. I was dead without being dead."

"I don't know what to say, Hagan," Daniel spoke. "You never heard from your family?"

"Never again," said Hagan. "But I have heard of Rapha. He is indeed evil and is indeed a giant and most certainly is lethal."

Daniel realized something about purpose at that moment. He stared straight ahead into the Valley of Eternity. "And I am going to have to kill him, aren't I, Hagan?"

"Yes, Daniel, you are going to have to kill my son."

CHAPTER 12

There would be battle in the morning. David's forces had marched south while Baal-Achbor's forces had marched north. Both armies camped across from each other outside the city of Beersheba.

In the tent surrounding King David was Joab, the commander of the army, Benaiah, Zalmon, and Abishai. These men had survived many battles and were proven warriors, and every one of them was hesitant about the battle plans. "I just do not feel comfortable with you leading the forces in the middle, my king," Benaiah spoke. For the strategy had been decided and would consist of King David leading the attack directly at the center of the Edomites. Benaiah would lead forces on the right and would attempt to outflank the enemy, while Zalmon would lead the forces in an attack on the left. Abishai would stay in reserve with ten thousand, ready to reinforce whichever of the three attacks needed it. Joab would take five thousand men and attempt to maneuver around the Edomites and lead a vicious attack from the rear.

Kind David again addressed his mighty warriors. "I know none of you are comfortable with me leading the center attack. But we must remember, this is not our battle, but is the Lord's. He will be with us and will fight for us and hold us up in His victorious right hand. For He will defend his people."

"My Lord King, you must allow four household guards to surround you and protect you during the battle," said Benaiah.

David answered, "I will allow Ishbaal the Tachmonite, Eleazer son of Dodo, and Shammah son of Agee to accompany and fight alongside me." These were perhaps the three mightiest warriors in all of Israel.

Zalmon said, "That is good, my king, for they will properly defend and fight well by your side."

"We will attack at dawn," King David declared.

The hordes of Namok were out in full force. Demons everywhere. Evil persisted throughout the Edomite camp. It almost seemed as if every Edomite soldier had a demon attached to him, whispering, speaking, and breathing evil into them. Lucifer had entered the spirit of King Baal-Achbor and was guiding every thought. He had taken over his mind and was directing the generals, preparing for the morning's attack from the Israelites.

In truth, Lucifer did not care if the Edomites won or lost this battle. The only thing he cared about was the death of King David. This was the culmination of years of planning and deception that had begun with the kidnapping of the half-human, half-angelic boy, Rapha. Rapha would be the one to kill King David and destroy the prophecy of the coming savior. This opportunity must not be wasted.

Rapha, Saph, Lahmi, and Ishbi had received their orders from Lucifer himself. Ishbi, the youngest giant, had already left and was inside the city of Jerusalem, preparing the city for the return of its dead king. Rapha, Saph, and Lahmi were preparing for the morning. Drinking heavily and being filled with evil that knew no bounds. This is what they had been trained to do. Kill and destroy. No feeling, no remorse, no mercy. Rapha was almost completely drunk as he lay back and allowed his mind to drift to the days of his childhood in Namok, the land of the demons. There was constant darkness, and fire was everywhere. The fires could never be satisfied and never seemed to get enough, always thirsting, always hungry for more. The only way Rapha could survive was to accept the evil and allow it to overtake him. Lucifer was his instructor and took responsibility for his survival. He taught Rapha that evil was good, and good was evil. He taught him that God was his enemy and was full of hatred toward him.

Rapha was just trying to survive and knew that in order to do this, he must accept everything that was being fed into him. After asking about his mother and father one time, Lucifer beat him mercilessly until Rapha believed he was about to die. Lucifer had a large red stick he carried with him and would swing like a sword. Over and over, the red stick pounded Rapha. In the head, on the back, into the stomach, across the face. "You do not ever ask or think about your mother or father. I am your mother and I am your father!" Any flame of goodness or righteousness that may have existed in the deepest part of his soul was extinguished forever.

There were no friendships in Namok. It was a place of torment. If Rapha were truthful with himself, he would admit that he hated it. Looking forward to being able to exist outside of Namok, Rapha grew rapidly and full of strength. He knew he was more powerful than almost any demon. Lucifer began to take him to different areas on earth. No matter the area, Lucifer always insisted Rapha kill, drinking the blood of his victims. Before he murdered his first family, there had been a slight hesitation, followed by a blast against his head with the red stick of Satan. Eventually, the hesitations were gone, and Rapha began to look forward to his kills.

Lucifer allowed the giant to settle in Haifa, unbeknownst to him, the place of his birth. It was in Haifa that the rapes began, and sons were born. Three sons, each born in Haifa, and each taken by Lucifer from the mother to Namok.

Rapha could not love. He loved no woman and did not even love his sons. He had been taught by the prince of darkness to never love. He existed only for evil and knew that his ultimate reason for existing was about to be realized with the killing of King David. Rapha would rest before the morning. He licked his lips, already tasting the blood of King David in his mouth.

CHAPTER 13

Hagan sensed that a battle was looming, and the defender realm would be called upon to fight for the Lord. He worried Daniel was not ready, believing he still needed more training. As they finished a session, Daniel was cleaning and sharpening Avigdor as Hagan gazed at him. What he saw was far from the twelve-year-old boy who rode into the Valley of Eternity many years ago. He saw a young man, strong, determined with the spirit of the Lord in him. Tall with broad, strong shoulders, graceful in all his movements, Daniel had the look of a fearsome warrior. His hair was long, and he had grown a beard. It was said that Daniel's facial features were almost identical to his father, King David.

Hagan thought about his son, Rapha, and wondered if there were any similarities they shared. What did Rapha look like? Did he resemble Sedena? Or did he resemble Hadrach? He knew he must be incredibly powerful and wholeheartedly evil and knew Daniel would need to use every bit of knowledge he had given him. Had he taught Daniel enough? Could he control his spirit when the battle-joy came upon him? Could he control Avigdor in the midst of a real battle, allowing the blade to become one with him?

Foremost on his mind was the question of whether he would be allowed to accompany the realm and fight in the battle against the demon-angels. Yes, he had been allowed to wield Breather of Life once again as he trained and mentored Daniel, but the question remained if he would be allowed to fight side by side with angels once again. Hagan had contemplated, asking Michael for permission but decided if the Lord needed him in the battle, he would be released from the valley at the appropriate time. Oh, how he yearned to be the Hagan of old.

"Daniel, the time is near, and I must finish my story before the coming battle," Hagan said to Daniel as they made their way back to the tree. "Obviously, I am no longer in the Abyss..."

Sitting atop the tree high above the valley, Hagan began, "I was in the Abyss for a long period of time. We do not have any real concept of time, but using your method, Daniel, I would suppose maybe somewhere around fifty years. I really have no idea, only that it was a long time. Floating in darkness, unable to move, alone. I could think and reason for a while, but soon my spirit and mind were paralyzed just like my body. Like I told you earlier, I was dead without being dead. In fact, it would have been easier for me to have died rather than to exist in the eternal darkness of the Abyss. Lucifer had delivered to me the ultimate punishment, total separation from any form of life. It was strange, the last thing I remember thinking before my mind totally went dark was just complete sadness. I say it was strange because angels do not feel emotions, but somehow, I remember feeling despair.

"Daniel, I deserved everything that had happened to me. I was responsible for my decision to follow Lucifer and join the rebellion. I had spread death and destruction upon the earth. I had chosen evil over good and had become an enemy of God. Yet, as Hadrach, I had also loved and repented and asked God to forgive me. It was Sedena and Boldak and their family that had helped me rediscover my love for God. Then it happened. I felt the hand. I was being lifted. Only God has the power to pull an angel, or any living thing, out of the Abyss. It was the Hand of God. I was in his palm and suddenly blinded by light. Not being able to see, I could hear, and I heard the voice of God.

"God spoke to me, Daniel. He said, 'Hagan, you are being restored. I forgive you. You will return to the Valley of Eternity, land of angels, and you will have purpose again.' And then He said the words I most needed to hear. 'Hagan, I created you and I love you.' God left, my eyes were opened, and I saw Michael, the archangel. 'Greetings, Hagan,' Michael spoke. 'I am to take you back to the Valley of Eternity, but first we must retrieve something.' My wings had been restored, although they were much smaller. In fact, they looked as they look today. I was no longer huge and powerful but was average height and slim, but I did not care, I had been rescued from the darkness, saved from the Abyss.

I followed Michael to the Gates of Namok.

"Next thing I knew, Lucifer was standing before us with thousands of demons all around. Michael spoke in a voice of authority, the voice of the angel of angels. 'Brother, we are here for the sword, the Breather of Life. You will return it to Hagan.' I expected Lucifer to refuse and to prepare to do battle with us. But, somehow, he knew that Michael was speaking for the Lord and that this was a command from God. The Breather of Life had been created by God and given to me. It would now be returned to me. Lucifer produced the blade and threw it at my feet. 'Next time, I will not throw you into the Abyss. I will sever your head. And I will use your own sword when I do it.' He added, 'I will also make sure your son and grandsons are watching when I do it.'

"I said nothing. Lucifer and Michael just stared at each other. I have long felt, Daniel, that these two brothers are destined to have an epic battle with each other at some point. They are both so powerful, I must confess when it happens, I do not know who will win. We traveled back to the Valley of Eternity, the bells ringing as Ishboth opened the gates to let us in. Michael, riding Pran, and me sitting directly behind him. I reentered the valley the same way you entered, Daniel, sitting behind Michael. The angels did not know how to respond to my return. The bells continued to ring for a long time.

"Angels looked at me, some giving a slight nod, others just stared. Michael delivered me to this tree. He set me down and said, 'Welcome home, Hagan. You will once again belong to the defender realm, training and teaching with them. However, you will not leave the valley again, and you will not be permitted to draw Breather of Life from its scabbard without permission from the Lord. Do you understand, Hagan?' 'Yes,' I said, 'thank you, Michael.' The Lord has allowed me to retain my memory of what happened. To remember Sedena and our love. I am thankful for that. He also has restored my purpose. To train you and to prepare you to become the defender I was never able to fulfill. That is my story, Daniel. It is now time for your story to begin. Prepare your spirit for battle."

CHAPTER 14

The chariots of Edom were both beautiful and fearsome. Baal-Achbor ordered his sixty war horses to the center of the army. The iron-wheeled chariots were built to cut terrible swathes through the ranks of their enemy. Quick and maneuverable, the chariots combined speed with stability. The horses were trained for battle, and the platform carried two Edomites, one being the driver, concerned only with controlling the horse, while the other was free to attack with sword and spear.

Normally, the Edomites would spread their chariots of war across the entire front line; however, Lucifer knew King David would come from the center, so the chariots would attack united, charging the oncoming king.

Dawn was almost here. As the sun peaked its head over the horizon, both armies were lined up and ready for battle. The air was crisp with a slight breeze blowing across the battlefield. This would be a day of death, not only in the physical world but also in the spiritual world. King David's army was surrounded by thousands of angels, white as far as the eye could see. Michael was there, seated on Pran, Uri close behind him.

King Baal-Achbor's army was likewise surrounded by hordes of demons, gathered from the depths of Namok to do battle with the angels of heaven. Lucifer exited the body of Baal-Achbor, rising into the sky to stand at the head of his demons. A feeling of euphoria pulsated throughout his body as he realized the day had finally arrived.

Today would mark the death of King David, the death of the prophecy, and also, the death of his brother, Michael.

Michael drew Tyrfing, held it high above his head and yelled, "The Lord is here and everywhere!" Michael charged.

King David had drawn the sword of Goliath, yelling, "For the Lord and for Abigail!" David and the Israelites charged the army of Edomites.

The battle had begun. Lucifer met the charge of Michael. Tyrfing clashing with Abaddon. As the demons and the angels battled all around, Lucifer and Michael fought. Michael was using his great power and strength as he went on the attack, hitting Lucifer with blow after blow. Lucifer was having trouble matching the speed of Michael and found himself struggling to fend off the mighty sword. As Michael fought, his eyes were fire, his hair flowing, and his mighty wings spread out toward the heavens. Pran had been released to do his own killing, running through the hordes of demons.

Lucifer began to feel the rhythm of Michael and his attack, feeling his evil growing stronger. Yet, he could not find any vulnerability in Michael. They were flying through the sky, each trying to find some weakness in the other. Tyrfing suddenly pierced the thigh of Satan, causing devil's blood to spurt. Michael followed with a stab into the shoulder, driving Tyrfing deep. Lucifer let out a satanic scream, dropping Abaddon from his hand. Lucifer went to his knees, staring up into the eyes of his brother. He began to laugh.

Michael grabbed the head of Satan, lifting Tyrfing for the deathblow. As he swung his sword with all his might, Lucifer transformed into the dragon, throwing Michael off balance. The dragon was enormous, four legs with claws and scales that were sharp as spikes, mouth full of razor-like teeth, and two horns protruding from the scalp. The dragon was red in color, but the tail black as coal and full of tiny sharp blades. The Red Dragon laughed again and spoke in the language of Enochian. "You surely did not think it would be that easy, did you, brother? You know nothing of my power, I have grown more dominant than you will ever know. I have become God!"

Regaining his balance, Michael stood and said, "You are no God. You have already been defeated. Whether you are one dragon or ten dragons, you cannot stand before the Lord. His righteousness cannot be defeated."

The dragon breathed the fire of Namok onto Michael, completely engulfing him and forcing him to retreat. Fire that would not subside, it just kept coming more and more forcefully. Though the fire did not burn Michael, the force kept him from advancing against the dragon. Michael waited, knowing that when the fire was done, he would fight and would kill the Red Dragon.

David was swinging his sword, the joy of battle returning to his spirit. It had been a long time since he stood and fought side by side with his men against an enemy trying to take his life. Fighting alongside Ishbaal, Eleazer, and Shammah, three of his mightiest men, David was fending off the charging chariots of war. The chariots just kept coming, a seemingly endless onslaught coming directly at him. Being a true warrior, the king knew death could come at any moment, but he fought in the spirit of the Lord, trusting that He would provide a great victory. By his side, he heard a great moan and turned to see a giant spike being driven through the belly of Eleazer. Eleazer fell, dead before he hit the ground, and King David came face-to-face with Rapha, the giant of giants. Rapha was covered with blood.

"Hello, King David, I have been waiting for this moment." Shammah wheeled and hit the giant from behind with all his force. Rapha turned and grabbed the mighty warrior by the throat. Shammah knocked his arm loose and began to engage sword to sword with Rapha. As the giant and Shammah battled, David was faced with another chariot coming directly toward him. The spear hit him through his left thigh causing the king to stumble and fall. Ishbaal called out but could not reach him for the piles of bodies all around him. The chariots just kept coming.

David was grabbed by the hair and dragged to his feet by giant Saph. Saph swung repeatedly at his head hitting him over and over with his fist. These were unlike any men David had ever seen before. Huge, brutal, they almost seemed as if they were not human. The king knew if he did not gain his release, he was doomed as he was just about to lose consciousness. The killing of the king had been reserved for Rapha; it was to be his honor to eat the heart and drink the royal blood; therefore, Saph was careful with his last blow. While Saph was concerned with preserving the life of the king, David reached into his breastplate, grabbed his dagger, and thrust it into the heart of Saph with all his might. "In the name of the Lord!" David yelled.

Saph stumbled, stunned at the quickness of David and the might of his thrust. He reached for the hilt of the dagger, pulled it from his heart, his half-human, half-angelic blood gushing all over King David. Reaching down and picking up the sword that had taken the head of Goliath all those years ago, David swung at the head of Saph. The head of the giant hit the ground. Blood everywhere. Rapha had finally cut the throat of Shammah and was drinking blood when he saw the head of his son rolling upon the ground. As Ishbaal rushed to the side of his king, giant Lahmi appeared and cut him off. "Your king is doomed, and you are doomed as well," Lahmi said.

Rapha reached down, knocked King David unconscious, scooped him up and carried him away from the battle. Lahmi drove his spear into the neck of Ishbaal before following his father out of the battle. The three mighty men, Eleazer, Shammah, and Ishbaal all lay dead on the battlefield, alongside the headless giant Saph. King David was gone.

The fire from the Red Dragon finally ended and archangel Michael charged, but Lucifer was gone, disappearing from the battle. Michael turned and fought with his fellow defender angels. The demon horde was still engaging the angels, and battles were going on all throughout the spiritual realm. The only way a demon could be killed was to have its head removed by an angelic blade. The same was true for angels, as the head must be removed by a demonic blade. Heads of demons and angels could be seen throughout the realm. Michael gave the signal, summoning his army of angels to gather. Pran returned, and Michael rested upon his back, blowing his horn once again for all angels to hear. The battle had been fierce, and the demons had proved to be a formidable opponent. Michael would withdraw and wait for instructions from the Lord. He knew his work was far from over. Lucifer was, indeed, strong and his evil was as great as it had ever been. His plan was in motion, and Michael knew the time had come for Daniel to emerge from the Valley of Eternity.

Lucifer was leading Rapha and Lahmi back to the city of Jerusalem. Rather than kill David immediately, he decided to first use him to draw out this young son of his who he knew had been training under Hagan in the Valley of Eternity. He would allow his giants to kill David and his "angel son" at the same time. Father and son would die at the hands of Rapha.

Rapha, still carrying David over his shoulder, felt no sadness or remorse for the loss of his son, Saph. Any love in his heart had been extinguished long ago. He lived now only to serve his Lord, Lucifer. Rapha wondered why they were leaving the battle and returning to Jerusalem. He could easily kill David at any moment, yet he had to obey and trust Lucifer.

King Baal-Achbor knew they were winning. The Israelites were in disarray. Their king had vanished, and three of their mightiest warriors were dead. Benaiah's attempt at outflanking the Edomites had been unsuccessful. Joab had encircled the Edomites and was attacking from the rear. Baal-Achbor realized if he could defeat and crush the rear attack, his Edomites would be in position to defeat the Israelites once and for all.

Michael rode through the gate of the Valley of Eternity. The Lord had given him instructions to take Daniel from the valley and lead him back to his home, back to Jerusalem. "It is time, Daniel. The Lord has purpose for you back in your former home," Michael said as he found Daniel and Hagan on the training ground next to the river of Hope. There would be no more training, no more lessons, no more mentoring. It was time for Daniel to take what he had learned from the valley and be the defender he was called to be.

Hagan prepared Daniel. He gave him leather armor to put on. "This will allow you to move quicker than your opponent. It may not be as protective as metal armor but will serve you better, allowing you more freedom in movement." Hagan helped Daniel put on the leather shin protectors as well as the leather armbands. "You will wear no helmet, for you are an angel now, and angels do not wear helmets." Avigdor was strapped around his waist. "You are ready, young defender."

Hagan stood face-to-face with Daniel. He realized he would not be permitted to leave the valley to accompany his protégé to Jerusalem. "It is goodbye for now, Daniel. You have learned your lessons well, and you have grown into a great warrior. You must now take what you have learned and use it. Remember, the battle is the Lord's, you are His instrument. Control your spirit, balance your body and your mind, become one with Avigdor. Do not allow fear to ever creep into your soul, do not be afraid to die, always fight with honor." Hagan placed his hand upon Daniel's shoulder. "I hope to be able to see you again, my defender."

Daniel had tears in his eyes. He loved Hagan, who had been a father to him. "I will make you proud of me, Hagan. Thank you for all you have done for me. I love you." Daniel stepped forward and gave Hagan a hug, holding onto him for a long time. "Goodbye, for now."

As Michael left the valley riding Pran, with Daniel seated behind him, Hagan called out one last thing to Daniel. "Remember, Daniel, always remember, you can fly!" And Michael and Daniel were gone.

CHAPTER 15

Giant Ishbi's job had been to prepare Jerusalem for the arrival of Lucifer, David, and the giants. Almost the entire army had left the royal city with the king, so it was easy work for Ishbi to kill the remaining guards and to gain access to the palace of King David. The women and children hid in their homes, immensely frightened of this eight-foot, five-hundred-pound giant.

The only woman he encountered was Lizona, the former maid servant to Abigail who had been beaten and raped by the giant brothers prior to Abigail's murder. Lizona had been allowed to serve in the king's household and was there when Ishbi arrived. She hid in her chamber listening to Ishbi attack and brutally kill all the servants and guards. Lizona tried to escape, sneaking out the back entrance to the palace, but she was discovered by the giant, who was standing just outside the rear entrance. The giant cornered Lizona, breathing his breath into her mouth. "I remember you. Hello again, my sweet girl. Did you bear no child from our first encounter?"

Lizona was frozen in fear and could not speak. "Speak!" yelled Ishbi.

"No, I did not," whispered Lizona.

"Well, we may need to try again, my sweetness," said the giant as he took his nasty tongue and licked it across the lips of Lizona. "But first, you must take me to the home of a woman named Bathsheba. You will lead, and I will follow, and please, do not try anything stupid or else you will feel nothing but my hand ripping out your heart."

Lizona led Ishbi the giant to the home of Bathsheba, wife of King David. Bathsheba was one of many wives to the king in Jerusalem, but she was the specific one Lucifer had asked for. The wife of the king was well-protected by guards, but as had been the case with Abigail, these guards were no match for a half-human, half-angelic deranged giant. Ishbi was taken aback when he gazed upon the beauty of Bathsheba. She had beautiful long brown hair, and her skin was unblemished. Brown eyes looked on in horror as she saw the face of evil staring at her. "What do you want with me?" asked Bathsheba.

"You will find out soon enough," replied Ishbi.

Ishbi grabbed Bathsheba. Kicking Lizona in the back, he told her to lead them back to the palace of David. Tying up Bathsheba and Lizona on the rooftop of the palace, Ishbi went to the southern gate of the city. This would be the gate Rapha would enter. He took torches and lined them up on both sides of the street that would lead to the palace. Lighting the torches, the entrance from the southern gate looked like an entrance into hell. As King David was forced into his city from the southern gate, Lucifer wanted him to see the fire and feel the doom and destruction that was about to overtake him.

The preparations were complete; the city was ready for Lucifer's arrival.

Ishbi was growing impatient. He wanted to be in the battle. The killing in the city of Jerusalem had been easy; he was frustrated, wanting to be challenged. He went to the rooftop and untied Lizona, dragging her down the stairway into the bedroom of the king. "I want to finish what we started, only this time I will plant a son into you." Maybe this would make him feel better, he thought. He ripped the clothes off Lizona, slapping her repeatedly across the face, she lay helpless and naked across the bed. Reaching for his own pants, he suddenly felt a hand grab him around his collar and ripped him backward with a force he knew not many could possess. Sprawling across the floor, the giant gathered himself, standing and facing something he had never seen before.

Standing across from Ishbi was Daniel, the defender of the Lord.

"You will not touch her again," said Daniel in a voice of authority.

"Who are you?" asked Ishbi. "I don't think you know what you are doing."

"My name is Daniel, son of David, defender of the Lord, and I have come this day for you, giant." Daniel drew Avigdor. "Today you will die."

Ishbi said, "But I do not have my sword. Are you going fight me with no sword? There is no honor in that."

Daniel replied, "Retrieve your sword and meet me outside the palace." As Ishbi left to gather his sword, Daniel followed him out the door. Before he had left the room, Lizona said, "Thank you, Daniel. Please be careful." Daniel turned, looked at Lizona, and felt something in his heart he had never felt before. He was not quite sure what it was, awkwardly nodding at Lizona as he left the room.

Ishbi sucker-punched Daniel as he walked out the front door of the palace. Daniel stumbled before regaining his footing. The giant charged toward him to hit him again. Sidestepping the punch, Daniel took his left hand and hit Ishbi across the nose with all his might, shattering the nose and bones in the face as blood began to spill out of his nostrils. "You know what I think you are, giant?" asked Daniel. "I think you are just a big bully who has never had to fight a warrior in a fair fight. Today you are about to feel the power of the Lord." Daniel hit him again, shattering more bones and crushing teeth.

Ishbi was much larger, but his size was no match for the strength and quickness of Daniel. Avigdor hammered down on the sword of Ishbi, each blow stronger than the previous. Without Rapha, Saph, and Lahmi there to help, Ishbi found himself struggling to survive for the first time in his life. Daniel spun to his left, avoiding a sword thrust and again swung his left hand at the head of the giant. The blow sent Ishbi to one knee.

Asmodeus arrived. Whispering into the ear of Ishbi, "Get up and fight! You must hold on until Rapha arrives, he and Lucifer are close. I am not permitted to fight him. You must do this! Grab his sword with your hand. It will cut you, but you must remove it from his hand and use your great size to your advantage."

Daniel swung Avigdor. Ishbi reached up at the last second and grabbed the sword with his hand. He squeezed the blade, allowing it to cut through the muscle of his hand. With all his strength, he ripped the sword out of Daniel's grasp, reaching for the throat with the other hand. Ishbi was squeezing the throat of Daniel, lifting him off the ground. Daniel could feel his life slipping away. His eyes went to the sky, and he saw his defenders gathered around watching. He saw Gad, Bildad, and Mahlon. Hundreds of others were there. He needed Hagan, needed to hear his voice and instruction. He could not get out of the giant's grip. All his training, all the teaching just to be choked out by the enormous hand of Ishbi. "Squeeze it! Crush his throat! End it!" shouted Asmodeus.

Lizona came from the palace carrying a large shovel. She rushed up behind Ishbi and swung with all her might at the calves of the giant, causing just enough of a distraction for Daniel to break free. Daniel was flying. His head clearing, his spirit being controlled, he flew through his angels back toward the giant who had turned toward Lizona in a rage. Ishbi was swinging his sword at the heart of Lizona as Daniel hit him solidly, knocking him to the ground. Flying to Avigdor, he grabbed the mighty sword and walked toward the stunned giant. "How can you fly, you have no wings, you are no angel?" asked Ishbi.

"You know nothing of my power," Daniel spoke as he went on the attack, Avigdor hungry for the blood of a giant. Avigdor's rage knocked the blade from the hand of the giant before entering the chest, ripping through the heart. Daniel pulled his blade free as the giant was on both knees gasping for air. "May your soul torment forever in Namok," Daniel said as Avigdor sliced the head from the body of Ishbi.

Asmodeus appeared to Daniel. "You will regret what you have done, son of David. The last thing your eyes will see upon this earth is the giant Rapha eating the heart and drinking the blood of your father, just like he drank the blood of your mother." Daniel stared at Asmodeus, wanting to engage him in battle. "That is right, I was there. I saw Rapha slice through your mother as she cried out for her poor little Chileab. Where were you on that day? Hagan did not tell you that, did he?"

The rage was filling inside of Daniel. He had been taught by Hagan not to ever engage a demon in battle. They were not allowed to harm him unless provoked. "You must control your emotions, Daniel, they will try to get you to attack, and then they will have permission and justification to destroy you. You must not fall into their trap," Hagan had told him many times.

"Daniel? Daniel?" Lizona was calling his name. Daniel took his eyes off Asmodeus, who suddenly fled.

Staring at Lizona, Daniel said, "It is my turn to thank you, Lizona. It has been a long time since we have seen each other."

Lizona responded, "I am glad you are back, Daniel. But I have some sad news to give you concerning your mother."

Daniel sat staring at Lizona as she told him about the day the giants came to see his mother. She told him every detail she could remember, crying as she recounted being raped by giants. Bathsheba put her arms around her. "There was nothing I could do, I was helpless. To this day, I cannot get the laughter of the giants out of my mind."

Daniel did not know what he could say that would bring comfort. He simply said, "I appreciate you telling me what happened, Lizona. The day will come when my mother will be avenged. Today was just the beginning." He left Bathsheba and Lizona alone to talk some more as he walked outside to where the giant's body and head still lay.

Picking up the head of Ishbi, he looked closely at the face. A face of evil. No feeling, no kindness. It was hard for Daniel to imagine that this giant was the grandson of Hagan. There were no similarities he could detect, though he had to remind himself he was not quite sure what Hadrach had looked like. There may have also been features of Sedena within the face.

Daniel found a pike and stuck the head of Ishbi on the tip, carrying it to the entrance of Jerusalem. Seeing the flames burning, he felt certain the arrival of Rapha was imminent. Good. The first thing he would see would be the head of his son on a pike. Rapha would soon regret the day he grabbed his mother and slit her throat.

Bathsheba and Lizona led Daniel to the burial tomb of Abigail. The people of Jerusalem were still frightened, staying inside their homes, fearful of the flames and what was to come. They did, however, look out of their doors and windows to get a view of this Daniel, whom most did not recognize as the son of the king. They saw a warrior with a beard and long hair. Tall and muscular, carrying a huge and mighty sword. Some were even saying he could fly; they had seen him in the air. He must be some sort of angel sent from the Lord for their protection against the giants. Word had spread he had killed one giant. Perhaps the Lord had heard their prayers.

Staring at the tomb of his mother, Daniel felt sadness in his spirit. His mother had loved him deeply. He was her Chileab, her pride and joy, and he had been taken from her, leaving her to live a life of loneliness. "I love you, Mother," Daniel whispered. He vowed that her death would not go unpunished, but he also knew what Hagan would tell him. Hagan would tell him not to ever allow emotion to cloud his purpose. "You must always fulfill your purpose. That is why you are here and being trained in the ways of the angel. Do not let feelings or emotion ever get in the way of what you must accomplish. Emotion will betray you and cause you to think irrationally."

Daniel turned and asked Lizona, "Do you know where my harp is?"

Daniel sat on the rooftop of his father's palace. He placed his fingers on the harp and closed his eyes. It had been so long since he had pulled the strings, he feared he might not remember the notes, but he wanted to play. He wanted to play for his mother. "In the Fields of Ancient Days" flowed from his fingers, the beautiful sounds ringing out into the evening air of Jerusalem.

Rapha and Lahmi stopped at the southern gate. They looked at the head of Ishbi. While Lahmi felt anger at seeing his brother's head displayed on a pike, Rapha felt nothing. He only wondered who had been able to defeat a giant. Two of his sons were now gone. "Prepare yourself," he told Lahmi.

David followed in chains. Looking at the head of the giant, he too wondered which of his warriors he had left behind had been able to slay a giant. It had been a brutal trip back to the city. Pulled, dragged, and beaten by Rapha along the way, he had believed he would be killed at any moment. Rapha wanted to kill him. He could sense that, but he also sensed he was being dragged back to his city for some reason. The king prayed. He prayed for his army back in the battle. The battle had not been going well. He asked the Lord to protect his people and give them a mighty victory. "Deliver me from evil, deliver me from my enemies, Lord, show your might and your glory to all the world."

"Shut up! Your life is not even worth saving!" Rapha said. "I will be eating your worthless heart very soon!"

Rapha could feel the presence of Lucifer approaching. The demons flew into Jerusalem by the thousands. The Red Dragon was leading his horde. Circling the city over and over, evil rested upon the city. Lucifer had ordered his demons to leave the Edomites and travel back to Jerusalem, forming a protective shield around Lucifer as he and the giants did what must be done.

Rapha and Lahmi, dragging the chains of King David up the street to the king's palace, stopped just short of the entrance. Lucifer appeared, speaking to Rapha, "The death of Ishbi has caused me to change our plans. The boy defender must be dealt with. We must ignite his emotion and give him reason to make a mistake. Unchain the king and send him up the path to the entrance of his palace."

Rapha unchained King David and told him to walk the path toward his palace. As David began the last hundred-yard march to his home, he looked up and saw Daniel standing in front of the palace. He immediately recognized him because it was as if he were looking into a mirror. Although larger and more powerful than himself, the facial features were almost identical. It was Daniel, and he was home. David could not believe how tall and powerful his second son had become. He was a warrior. David began to trot the last few paces to embrace his son. Daniel saw the spear, lifted and released by Rapha. "Down, down, get down, Father!" Yet, Daniel was yelling in Enochian, and David did not recognize what he was saying until it was too late. Ten yards before he would embrace his son, the spear of Rapha pierced through the back of King David. Bathsheba was screaming as she watched from the rooftop.

David fell. The angels were suddenly all around. Demons and angels began to battle. Angelic swords clashing with demonic blades. Daniel lost all self-control and charged at Rapha. Michael rode Pran into the city, scooping up the body of David. Rapha and Daniel fought.

Daniel knew as he swung Avigdor this was no ordinary giant. For this was the son of Hagan, the giant of giants. He would not fall as easily as Ishbi. "I have been waiting for this day," said Rapha as he deflected the blows of Daniel. Lahmi came up behind Daniel as he found himself facing two giants. "Breath, control, remember what you have learned," Daniel could almost hear the words of Hagan. "Fly!"

Daniel was in the air as both giants swung at the same time, missing. He came down behind Rapha, slamming Avigdor into his shoulder. The blow had no effect as Rapha said, "I hope you have more than that, little boy." Daniel had decided he would concentrate on the more dangerous Rapha and try to stay away from Lahmi. In the air again, deliver the blow, back in the air. Over and over. Rapha had no weaknesses!

Avigdor was the superior sword and went to work attacking the big giant, but each thrust was deflected by Rapha, who was talking the whole time. "Little man! I have killed thousands! Piece of turd! Challenge me!" His strength was incomprehensible, even as Avigdor delivered a clean thrust into the chest of the giant, the sword could not penetrate deeper than an inch. Rapha just grew angrier. It was as if Daniel was fighting Satan himself. What would Hagan do? How would Hagan attack this giant, his son? The warrior-defender must continue to use his quickness, get in the air, attack from all points. Hagan would tell him, "Stop thinking so much, you are reacting, trust your skills and act!"

Rapha's wrath burned hotter and hotter. "Give me your sword, Lahmi!" the giant screamed at his son. Lahmi tossed his sword to Rapha who now fought with two swords. It was too much for Daniel. Daniel parried desperately and tried to counter the dual swords, but Rapha pressed without yielding, never giving Daniel a chance to recover. As Daniel was backing away, Lahmi hit him from behind with a blow to his head. Dropping one of his swords, Rapha followed with his own blow to the head.

The giant's blow hit Daniel directly in the temple. He went down. It seemed as if the lights were fading. The faint sound of hoofbeats were ringing in his ears. Was that a horse? He was scooped up just before he passed out. Uri had reached down and grabbed the young warrior-defender.

Rapha raged. "Coward! Coward! Come back little coward!"

Daniel had escaped. The Lord had sent Uri to save the young warrior-defender. The demons gave chase as Uri rode his stallion at lightning speed. "Ishboth, open the gate!" Suddenly, Uri and Daniel were back in the Valley of Eternity. Ishboth shut the gate. The demons knew they could not pursue any further.

CHAPTER 16

Lucifer was enraged.

The red stick of Lucifer hit Rapha in the back of his head, causing him to lean over. Lucifer hit him again and again, blood beginning to pour from his right ear. The dragon's tail appeared, and Lucifer swung it around the neck of Rapha, choking the life out of the half-human, half-angelic monster.

Lucifer had given chase to Michael and David. He did not know if the spear had killed the king, thereby destroying the prophecy. If David was not dead, certainly he was near death. Lucifer must be certain, though. But he could not keep up with Pran, who blazed across the skies and lost them high above the Mediterranean Sea. Lucifer was almost as mad at himself as he was at Rapha. He should have just ordered Rapha to behead the king when he had the chance. He had allowed himself to become too overconfident and too preoccupied with the warrior-defender boy. The two angelic horses, ridden by Michael and Uri, had robbed him of two certain kills.

"You should have killed the boy! Are you so weak that two of you could not kill a boy?" Lucifer squeezed the neck of Rapha. "You are as worthless as your father! Give me one reason why I should not take the life from you right now!" Lucifer continued to berate Rapha, "You better hope your spear was successful at taking the life of David. If I find out otherwise, you are finished! I raised you, taught you, trained you for this moment, and you have failed." Lucifer released the tail from the neck of Rapha, the giant lying on the ground gasping for air. "You are a worthless piece of shit." Lucifer spit dark saliva all over the face of Rapha. "Do not fail me again, or it will be the end of you!" Turning to Lahmi, the prince of darkness said, "Go, bring me the woman Bathsheba and the handmaiden Lizona."

He had never seen the Satan so incensed. Rapha lay upon the ground for many minutes, motionless. Satan was his Lord. He had always served at the pleasure of Lucifer. In all his years, Rapha had never heard Lucifer mention anything about his father. As far as he was concerned, Lucifer had always been his father. Rapha had never wondered or even wanted to know who his real father was.

Until now.

The Edomites had every advantage. Successfully penetrating the center of the Israelite army, killing the mighty soldiers that surrounded their king, fending off the attack on their flank, and crushing the advance from behind. King David had disappeared, and the Israelite army was reeling, kingless, and retreating toward Jerusalem. Bodies lay everywhere. King Baal-Achbor would continue to press his advantage, pushing the decimated Israelites back toward their city where the Edomites would crush them once and for all.

Mahlon had been assigned his task. He must defend Bathsheba, the wife of King David, along with Lizona, servant in the palace of the king. He had received his instructions that he was to appear before the women and lead them to a place of safety. "Greetings, women of the Lord. I am to lead you to safety. You must follow me." Bathsheba and Lizona were scared, hiding in the attic of the king's palace. Mahlon had appeared through the walls, seemingly out of nowhere. As he led the women out of the palace through the darkness, they could hear the scream of Lahmi as he was destroying the palace piece by piece. "Quickly now, we are going underground."

To the old rock quarry hidden beneath the city of Jerusalem, Mahlon led Bathsheba and Lizona.

Adoni's cave. The hidden quarry had been a center of legend for hundreds of years. "Is this Adoni's cave?" Bathsheba asked Mahlon.

"Yes," replied the angel, "you will be safe here until the Lord calls for our return."

King Adoni had been an ancient king of Jerusalem when the mighty Joshua had invaded, taking the city for God's people. The king and his advisors were hidden in the quarry for many months before being discovered by Joshua and his army. Refusing to exit out of the quarry, legend said that the Lord turned the king and all his advisors into stones. It would be among these stones that Bathsheba and Lizona would hide from the giant.

Lightness emanated from Mahlon as he guarded the entrance to the cave. No one could enter without having to fight the defender. "What will we eat and drink? How are we going to survive down here?" asked Lizona.

"The Lord will provide for your needs," said Mahlon.

Just as Mahlon had declared, the next morning, stones had turned into bread, and water dripped from the wall, gathering into a small pool. "Why is the Lord doing this for us?" asked Bathsheba.

"Both of you are very important to King David and to the king's son, Daniel. There are plans for your lives, plans that will not altered by the evil of this world."

Bathsheba had to ask, "Does this mean that the king is still alive? He survived the spear of the giant?"

Mahlon turned and said to the women of the Lord, "Yes, the king has survived."

Michael had pulled the spear from the body of David as he lay across the back of Pran. Near death, the king was still breathing as Pran descended upon Eretria, a small port city located on a Greek peninsula in the Aegean Sea. David was barely conscious as he heard the voice of the archangel speaking to someone. "The Lord sends his greetings. He asks that you care for the king of Israel and help him regain his strength. You will be protected and will not be hindered in any way. As you have been guarded these many years, the Lord will continue to keep you hidden from the enemy. I will return for the king, and at that time, Rafaella will have a decision to make."

"Thank you," the lady spoke to Michael. "We will care for the king and return him to strength and wait for your return."

"Peace be with you," Michael said. With those words, Michael climbed on the back of Pran and disappeared into the heavens.

Still in and out of consciousness, King David felt himself in powerful arms, being carried inside a cottage-like building and laid upon a soft bed. For many days, the king was unconscious as his wounds were cared for, being treated with yarrow, goldenrod, and calendula.

On his fifth morning, David opened his eyes and could see clearly for the first time since the spear went through him. The air was cool, and he could hear the sea banging into rocks outside the room. His eyes went to the window, and he saw the clouds and the blue sky, feeling the breeze blowing into the room. The door opened, and David saw a woman enter carrying a tray of food. The woman was probably well into her sixties, but her hair showed no trace of gray, black as coal. Her skin was olive, and she moved with the grace and dignity of a woman with great wisdom. Her presence was easy-going, and her eyes were kind. She smiled. "Good morning, King David, it is good to see you are feeling better this day."

David was staring into the eyes of Sedena. "Where am I? What happened?" asked the king.

"There will be time for that, but first you must eat. Your body needs some nourishment as it rebuilds its strength. Eat and rest some more. Perhaps this evening I can share what I know of your story," Sedena warmly told the king. David ate, not realizing how hungry he had become. After the meal, he again was asleep.

Late in the afternoon, Sedena was again by the bedside of David, applying the afternoon dose of yarrow and goldenrod. David woke, feeling the herbs soaking into his wound. "Am I going to survive?" he asked Sedena.

"Oh yes, you are going to return to full strength. The Lord is not yet done with you, King David of Israel."

David looked at Sedena, "The Lord? Do you worship Yahweh, the God of Israel?"

"I do, He is my God and my family's God," Sedena said as she stood to leave. "I will be back shortly with your meal, and we will talk."

David heard swords banging into each other. He sat up and rolled out of the bed. He felt the pain in his chest and back and was unsteady as he made his way slowly to the window. He could not believe what he saw as he looked out into a courtyard. There was sword training taking place. A young boy was parrying and receiving instruction from the most amazing creature David had ever laid eyes upon. Another giant.

This giant was different. She was different. She was huge, at least eight feet tall, long black hair, powerful arms and legs. It seemed to David that she was about the exact size of the giant Rapha who had thrust his spear through his back. But as nasty, ugly, and evil as Rapha was, this giant was the total opposite. She turned and saw David looking at her, and she smiled. The smile was identical to the smile of the woman who had been tending his wounds. This giant was beautiful. A slight knock on the door, and Sedena entered carrying more food. "I see you are watching my daughter. She is quite amazing. I am sure you have never seen anything like her."

"I have seen giants. The wound you are treating was caused by a giant. But I have never seen one that was…well, that was…a…"

"That was a girl?" Sedena helped him finish his statement.

"Yes, that was a girl, a beautiful girl," David finished. "What is her name?"

"Her name is Rafaella," Sedena said.

David looked at Sedena and contemplated whether to bring up the similarities between the two giants, each about the same size, each with a name similar to the other. Rafaella and Rapha. He decided to speak, "The wound I have was caused by a giant named Rapha thrusting his spear at me as I ran to greet my son, Daniel. Rapha is the personification of evil. He is a murderer and destroyer, an enemy to God."

"I know, King David," Sedena said as tears welled in her eyes. "He is also my son.

"My name is Sedena, and I am the mother of giants."

Sedena sat at the bedside of David and told him how he came to be in Eretria. "You were brought here on a mighty horse ridden by a mighty angel. A spear had been thrust through your back, and the angel asked me to care for you and help you regain your strength. He said he would return to take you back to your home. It is my understanding that you are a king."

"Yes, I am David, the king of Israel and Judah. Are we far from these countries?" asked David.

"We are on a Greek peninsula jetting out into the Aegean Sea. My family was brought here by a merchant many years ago. I was a young mother who had just given birth to twins. Twin giants. We lived in a region called Haifa, a port village located southwest of Damascus on the Mediterranean Sea. It is about a two-day journey from your city of Jerusalem."

"Yes, I am familiar with Haifa, there are many followers of the Lord living in the region. Why were you brought to Eretria?" asked David.

Sedena hesitated to speak. She was not certain she should share her story with this king from a faraway land. Yet, she also felt a strange sensation within her soul that this king David and her life were somehow connected. There was a reason the angel had brought him here. Taking a deep breath and looking into the eyes of David, she said, "What I am about to share with you will be difficult for you to believe. I ask you to listen, and I ask you to believe, for it is all true."

Sedena spoke from her heart. She told of Hadrach and their love for each other. She shared the story of Hadrach being an angel named Hagan, a follower of Satan who repented from his evil to become a follower of God. The happiness of the pregnancy, the time of the birth, and the kidnapping of her son, Rapha, by an evil angel. She had never been able to see her son nor hold him, as he was immediately stolen from her arms. She never saw her husband again and could only assume he was killed by Lucifer. She birthed a daughter as well. "I do not think the evil angels were aware there were two infants inside of me. I thank my God every day Rafaella was spared and allowed to remain with me. My father, my three sisters, Rafaella and I were taken out of Haifa and smuggled to Eretria where we have lived ever since. There is no doubt in my mind the Lord has protected us all these years, allowing us to prosper in this place. He has kept us hidden from the evil that lurks the earth.

"My father, his name was Boldak, passed away several years ago, and my sisters have all married into fine Greek families. It is just Rafaella and I that live here and, as you have seen, my daughter teaches and trains local youth in the art of war. She is mighty warrior, I know. I am thankful she has chosen to remain here, yet I am in constant fear for her future."

"You never married or loved again?" asked King David.

"No, although it was for a very brief period, I loved Hadrach with all of my heart, and I know I could never love that way again. The purpose of my life has been to love God and to love Rafaella."

"When I told you of Rapha, it appeared you knew about him," David said. "What have you heard about your son?"

"Being a port city here in the Aegean Sea, we are surrounded by travelers who sail the world. We hear news from lands near and far. For many years, we have heard of giants who were great killers. I have heard the name of Rapha and his three sons, Saph, Ishbi, and Lahmi. It is strange to think that these are my grandsons. Rafaella has heard the tales and knows of the evil flowing in her brother. I have not kept it from her."

"Does it trouble her, knowing about Rapha?"

"Very much. She loves the Lord with all her heart and is deeply troubled her twin is overcome with wickedness. I think she would like to see him and face him and try to save him. I have told her many times, though, if she leaves this place, I fear for her safety."

David looked at the ground. "I am afraid I do not believe there is any feeling at all in the heart of Rapha. I need to tell you, Sedena, he murdered my wife, Abigail. He slit her throat and drank her blood. He is obsessed with killing me. Rapha has raped and murdered and destroyed for so long, I do not think there is any light in him at all. My advice for Rafaella would be to stay here far away from the evil. I need to tell you something else, Sedena. Two of the giants are gone. I killed Saph in battle fighting against an army of Edomites. I stabbed him in the heart and cut his head from his body. The giant named

Ishbi is also dead, and I think he died at the hands of my son, Daniel. My son has become a mighty warrior, taken from his mother Abigail as a young boy and trained by angels in heaven."

"Trained by angels?" Sedena asked.

"Yes, he was taken at the age of twelve by angels. I have not seen him for many years until the day when I was wounded. I saw my son and was running toward him when Rapha thrust his spear. Daniel has become strong and mighty."

Sedena and David sat together for a long time without speaking. It was as if their minds were digesting the things each had learned. The sound of sword on sword began again in the courtyard as Rafaella began another training session. After a long period of silence, David finally spoke. "Sedena, do you know what I think? Please do not take this the wrong way or think bad of me for saying it, but it almost seems as if my son has been trained by angels to kill your son, who has been trained by demons. It is not your fault Sedena, but Rapha is pure evil, I believe he must die."

She began to cry. Tears of sadness. For Rapha. For Hadrach. For that day many years ago when her son and her husband had been taken from her. The tears would not stop coming. Sedena knew King David was right. Rapha must die. She finally managed the words through her tears, "I know what you say is the truth. My son is evil. But I still believe there is goodness buried in there somewhere. It may be buried so deep that it can never be recovered, but as his mother, I must believe it still exists. He has the blood of angels in him, the blood of his father, Hagan the warrior-defender. I just want him to know there are people that love."

"I am sorry, Sedena, I respect your love for him as his mother, but Rapha is a beast. There is no love in him whatsoever. I must do everything in my power as the King of Israel and Judah to make sure he dies, paying for all the evil he has done throughout his life.

There is no way one so full of wickedness could ever be forgiven," the king said.

As David grew stronger over the weeks, he began to spar with Rafaella, slowly regaining his strength and skills. She was an excellent teacher and taught the king a new style of fighting, one with a lighter sword and no armor. Using lightweight, flexible swords, Rafaella believed in stabbing and slashing using lightning speed, which seemed unusual to David because of the huge strength of Rafaella.

"Oh, I can use a heavy sword and place the emphasis on my size and strength if needed, but I just prefer the speed of a lighter sword," Rafaella answered when questioned by David. "My ultimate goal is to become a master in all styles of swordsmanship."

During the evening meals, David mesmerized Sedena and Rafaella with stories from his youth. He talked of the many lonely hours he spent as a shepherd boy caring for his flock of sheep. Telling how he would graze the sheep, leading them to areas of good forage all the while keeping an eye out for poisonous plants and dangerous animals. Whenever he had a sheep that continuously strayed from the flock, David would use his staff to break the animal's leg. He would then bind the break and carry the sheep upon his shoulders while the wound heeled.

"Wouldn't the sheep be scared of you or even angry at you for breaking his leg?" asked Sedena.

"Actually, it would learn that I could be trusted. You see, the sheep needed me for everything while it healed. Food, transportation, protection. Once the animal was healed, it would be completely loyal to me, never straying again."

David told how God would speak to him during those lonely days and nights. "I knew I was being prepared for a great purpose. I could feel the spirit of the Lord upon me. I could feel his presence and hear his voice. As I look back on my youth, I now realize this was the time when God was preparing me for the events that would come later in my life. He taught me how to trust him and rely on him and not be fearful when faced with dangerous situations. I was continuously running off or killing coyotes, wolves, and foxes. I have even killed lions and bears who attempted to steal my animals. All of that is what helped prepare me to face Goliath."

Of course, David had to tell the story of his great victory over Goliath. Both Sedena and Rafaella had heard of the legendary battle. Rafaella was particularly interested in Goliath and what he was like. "He was definitely huge and powerful but was much more of a pure brute than you and your brother. He did not possess the quickness or agility or intelligence that seem to mark you and Rapha and your nephews. But he was indeed fearsome, standing a little taller than you, Rafaella, and he was extremely reliant on his armor and sword. He wore a helmet and had all this heavy armor. I can even remember his legs were covered with bronze protection. On his back, he carried a huge bronze javelin, and his spear was the finest spear I had ever seen. He was full of insults, berating me and calling me every name he could think of but then he started insulting the Lord with filthy, vulgar insults. When he started hurling the insults at God, it was then I knew I would be victorious. I just did not believe the Lord would allow him success over me. I told him that I was coming for him in the name of the Lord. I took my slingshot and planted a stone directly into his forehead. One stone. He fell. I was not sure if he was dead, so I took his sword and cut his head off. In fact, I kept the sword and have used it in many battles, including our recent fight with the Edomites. The sword that cut the head from Goliath is the same sword that cut the head from Saph. I am not sure where it is now, I would assume Rapha has it."

"You said Rapha was obsessed with killing you, King David. Why? Why do you think he wants you dead so badly?" asked Sedena.

"All of that, I am not sure, Sedena. I keep going back to what I said about knowing God has a mighty purpose for my life. Perhaps I still have not achieved that purpose. Maybe there is something Rapha and the evil that lives in him are trying to prevent me from achieving. I just have to trust in the Lord."

The home was quiet, and all were asleep when Rafaella entered the room of her mother. "Mother, mother," she whispered into her ear. Sedena rolled over to see her daughter hovering above her. "Can we talk, Mother? I feel as though the king has regained almost all of his strength, and the mighty angel will be coming soon to return him to Jerusalem," said Rafaella. "Mother, I have made a decision. I wish to travel to Jerusalem to see my brother."

Sedena knew deep in her heart that this moment would come. That Rafaella would want to venture out into the world to find her way, to experience her destiny. She also knew she could not deny her daughter this right. Rafaella had always been a faithful and obedient daughter. The spirit of the Lord was upon her, and the time had come for her to leave her home in Eretria. "I understand, my dear daughter," Sedena said. "I know you need to see the world and what is out there, but I am afraid you may not like what you see. The world is full of evil and wickedness. I fear for your safety, for the evil one will attack you with all of his strength."

"Mother, we cannot live in fear. We must trust in the Lord, that He will protect me and fight for me and defend me. I feel the Lord is calling me to go and stand before my brother and look into his eyes and try to penetrate his soul, to share God's love with him. Yes, I may be disappointed, but I must try, Mother. I love you with all of my heart," Rafaella continued, "and this is my home and will always be my home. I will return to you, Mother, but this I must do at this time. I will make a promise to you. I promise I will not fight Rapha. I will not kill him, and if I cannot reach his heart, I will depart from him."

Sedena grabbed her daughter's hand. "You must be careful, Rafaella. You will be unlike anything anyone has ever seen before, a beautiful giant full of love and honor. Be on your guard, and if you are forced to battle, protect yourself and use all your power and all your strength and fight in the name of the Lord. I will be in prayer for you every moment of every day, my sweet daughter."

Sedena and Rafaella embraced. After Rafaella left the room, Sedena prayed to the Lord, "Please Lord, protect Rafaella. Do not let evil overtake her as it has overtaken my son. If there is any way you could use her to reach Rapha, please Lord, if there is any way you could forgive Rapha…"

Three days later, Michael returned. He sat upon Pran. Uri was with him, sitting atop his horse while a third riderless horse followed. Michael and Uri did not announce their arrival, did not knock or call out, but simply sat patiently outside the home of Sedena and Rafaella. It was David who spotted the angels. He opened the door, and Michael said, "Greetings, King David. We have come to return you to your home, Jerusalem. We trust you have regained your strength."

"Yes, I am ready, let me say goodbye to the women who have helped me."

At that moment, Sedena and Rafaella appeared. Rafaella was fully dressed in a long brown robe with her sword tied around her waist. Another blade hung upon her back. She had sandals and was carrying a small bag. Her long black hair had been braided and was pulled back into a ponytail that hung down her back. Obviously prepared to travel, David looked at her and said, "I take it you are wanting to travel with us?"

Sedena spoke directly to Michael. "Please allow my daughter, Rafaella, to travel with you and the king back to Jerusalem."

Michael already knew this request was coming and had been instructed by the Lord to allow the giant to travel with the king. "She is welcome to travel with us."

King David gave Sedena a warm hug and thanked her for all she had done for him. He told her he would never forget her kindness. Telling her he hoped to see her again one day, David climbed aboard the third horse, waiting for Rafaella.

Rafaella and Sedena embraced. "I love you, my daughter. May God go with you and protect you and use you for a mighty purpose." Rafaella could not speak, she had no words. She hugged her mother goodbye, climbed aboard the third horse behind David, and, suddenly, without warning, Michael, Uri, David, and Rafaella were gone, swept up into the sky, disappearing into the east. It was then that Sedena let the tears come. She cried uncontrollably, falling to her knees, then prostrate upon the ground. The last piece of her life was gone. First Hadrach, then Rapha, and now Rafaella. Gone. Alone in her despair, she wanted to cry out to her Lord and ask again that He would protect her daughter, but the words simply would not come. Only tears.

CHAPTER 17

The Israelite army set camp outside of the city of Lachish, located just southwest of Jerusalem. There would be no more retreating; the Edomites had caught them and were directly behind them. They would not make it to Jerusalem. The fight for the survival of the army would take place in Lachish.

Benaiah and Joab had led the army in retreat. No one knew for sure what had happened to the king. Rumors were flying. Some say he had been kidnapped and was being held by the Edomites, others said he had been killed and his body dragged off by the giants, while still others believed he had escaped and made it back to Jerusalem. Joab knew his king well, having fought many battles alongside him. He believed David was still alive and had escaped back to Jerusalem after killing the giant. David would be waiting for the army to return. Unfortunately, that scenario was not going to happen, thought Joab, as their fate was about to be decided once and for all. Badly defeated, with thousands killed in the first battle with Edom, the army was now outnumbered three-to-one and faced certain defeat when the war chariots attacked them in the morning.

Joab and Benaiah prepared the troops for the coming battle. They would fight with honor and, if need be, die with honor. Prayers were lifted out of the camp toward the heavens. Perhaps the Lord would hear their pleas and answer their prayers with a great victory. It was Benaiah's idea to attack the Edomites just before dawn. To take the battle to the enemy, to charge the chariots and take them by surprise. Outnumbered though they may be, the Israelites would blow the horn and charge the enemy and let the Lord have the results. Blood would flow at first light.

The angels surrounded the army of Israel. The demons surrounded the army of Edom.

It had been hard for Daniel to face Hagan. He felt like a failure; he had been defeated by Rapha and Lahmi. He had let Hagan down, and had it not been for Uri rescuing him, Daniel knew he would be dead. He felt as though he deserved to be dead. Why had Uri saved him?

Daniel stood in front of Hagan with his head down and tears in his eyes. He could not look his mentor in the eyes. Hagan spoke, "Tell me what happened."

Daniel, with head down, told Hagan about the battle with Ishbi, how he had been in the grasp of the huge giant until Lizona had distracted him with a blow to his calves. The distraction was all he needed to finally fly and let loose on the attack. Avigdor had taken the head of the giant, after which he had stood face-to-face with Asmodeus. Daniel told Hagan how deeply he wanted to fight Asmodeus after what he had told him about his mother. He wanted to engage the demon and avenge his mother.

"It was right not to engage Asmodeus," Hagan told him. "He is very powerful, second only to Lucifer, and I fear he may have been too much for you at that time. Your emotions had begun to temper your judgement. I am proud of you for resisting the urge to fight the demon. The time will come when you will fight demons, young one, but this was not the time."

Daniel finally raised his head, looked at Hagan through the tears, and asked, "Why did you not tell me about my mother? Did you know what Rapha and his sons did to her? You should have told me."

"Yes, I am aware of your mother's death. I am also aware that your mother is in heaven this very minute. Her earthly body was destroyed by Rapha, but she is very much alive with her heavenly body. It would have served no purpose for me to tell you about your mother's death. You would have been emotional and angry, and it would have severely interrupted your training. Remember, Daniel, you have a purpose, and you must not let emotion get in the way of your purpose. People live and people die, your purpose must never be affected by emotions. You serve the Lord."

"I am not an angel, Hagan, I have feelings."

"You are an angel, Daniel, you are the warrior-defender, trained to defend the Lord's people. You are as much of an angel as I am."

"But I cannot defeat Rapha. He is too powerful."

"You are wrong, young one, you can fight against even the strongest. We have but little time before you must return, but allow me to show you," Hagan said as he led Daniel to the training ground

As Hagan was flying to the training area, he closed his eyes and brought a prayer to the Lord. "Lord, I thank you for all you have done for me. Thank you for allowing me the privilege of training Daniel. You brought me back from the Abyss when I did not deserve it. Everything you have done for me I know I have not deserved. Yet, I bring one last request to you."

Hagan and Daniel landed upon the training ground. "Draw your sword, Daniel," said Hagan. "I am about to show you how to fight against power and might." Hagan lifted his eyes to the skies above the Valley of Eternity. "Lord, I ask you to give me my original form, to return my original strength, to present my original glory so that I may show young Daniel that he can fight against might. I ask that I might serve you once again as Defender of Defenders, not for me or my glory, but for you and your kingdom and your people. Let the valley see Hagan, and let Daniel see the true God-created power of the defender!"

Lightning crashed and thunder roared. Smoke filled the valley. There were not many angels in the valley, as most were in the army surrounding the Israelites, but the ones that were present looked on as Hagan returned to the angel God had originally created him to be. Daniel watched as he became large and mighty with muscles bulging out of arms and legs, white wings spread far and wide. His hair became golden and flowed all the way down his back. A golden headband could be seen upon his forehead, and a golden breastplate shone with a brightness that illuminated his entire being. Golden sandals were on his feet with silver shin guards strapped up almost to his knees. His forearms too were covered with silver. Daniel could still see the old Hagan in the face, especially in the eyes, but his features were now much sharper as he commanded a presence of authority. The only angel Daniel had seen that compared to Hagan was Michael, the archangel.

Hagan drew Breather of Life and said to Daniel, "You will fight me, and you will see that you are more powerful than you believe."

Breather of Life came down in an instant, Daniel barely raising Avigdor in time to meet the blow. "Let your emotions leave you, just fight!"

Throughout the valley, the two flew doing battle. Hagan was the much more powerful and skillful fighter, but Daniel seemed to grow in confidence each time he turned back an attack. He was growing up right before the eyes of Hagan. There was no emotion, no thought, no feelings; Daniel was fighting with purpose, striving to survive the onslaught from Hagan, who held nothing back. Daniel truly believed Hagan was trying to kill him and realized this was no ordinary training. A fight for survival.

Daniel spun and thrust Avigdor at the chest of Hagan, barely missing to the right; he spun again, this time to the left and thrust again. Breather of Life parried the blow and then slashed a quick strike at the left cheek of Daniel, cutting from beneath the eye down to the lower jaw, blood began to flow from the cheek. Hagan stopped. "A scar for you to remember you battled the great Defender and held your own." As Hagan was speaking, Avigdor was flying at his left shoulder. Hagan was not quick enough to stop the blow as Avigdor struck and cut just beneath the armor down the triceps of the angel. It was not a deep cut, and angels do not bleed, but it left enough of an impression that it could be considered a scar. "A scar for you to remember you battled Daniel, the warrior-defender, and held your own."

Angels rarely laugh. But Hagan and Daniel just looked at each other and laughed. Hagan had returned, and Daniel had grown up. They heard the horn being blown by Ishboth, the gatekeeper. Daniel was being summoned to leave the valley. Another horn. Hagan too was being summoned. It was time for Daniel and Hagan to fight by each other's side against the forces of evil. Out of the valley they flew.

Sedena was distraught, feeling all alone in Eretria. She was happy, for her sisters and the families each had grown, and she thought about visiting, but knew her mind would be with Rafaella in the faraway city of Jerusalem. She was an old woman now, and not sure how many years of life remained. After fasting and praying for three days, Sedena made her decision. Composing her request and signing it "from your old friend," Sedena hired a young boy from the village to deliver the message to the ports. She instructed the boy to find the man named Gadir and deliver the message to his hands. Gadir was an old man, and it had been many years since they had seen each other, but Sedena knew he and his sons still operated ships in the port.

A week passed. A knock on the door. Sedena opened, and there was Gadir, a huge smile upon his face. After embracing, Gadir said, "Obviously, I received your request. Have you thought this through clearly? We barely escaped that area those many years ago. Are you sure you want to return?"

"Yes, Gadir, I have prayed about it. There is nothing left for me here anymore. My daughter has traveled to Jerusalem, and I wish to join her there."

"There is war in the land," said Gadir. "The Edomites are at war with the Israelites. I do not think the area is safe for travel. It would be extremely dangerous for you, Sedena, I advise against it until the war is over."

"I have made my decision, Gadir, and I am asking for your help."

Gadir could tell from the determined look in Sedena's eyes that there would be no changing her mind. He also knew if he refused her request, she would search for another. There were many dishonest merchants and ships that Gadir knew would not be safe for her to travel. "Okay, my dear friend, I will arrange for your passage. I am an old man now and no longer can travel the seas, but I will have two of my sons prepare to deliver you to the port in Haifa. I know honest men there and will make sure you have safe passage from Haifa to Jerusalem."

"Thank you so much, Gadir. I am forever grateful."

"Please stay safe, my lady, and please return to us. Your presence will be missed here in Eretria," Gadir said as he gave Sedena another warm embrace. "My son, Nubia, will arrive here within the week to escort you to your ship. Goodbye, my friend."

As Gadir left, Sedena was filled with the thought that she would never see Gadir again. She would never see this home again. Exactly where her path east was taking her, she was uncertain, but one thing she was quite sure about. She would never return to Eretria.

CHAPTER 18

Michael and Uri delivered the king and Rafaella to the southern gates of Jerusalem. "You will find your army ten miles south of here preparing to fight the Edomites. You may keep the horse and ride to the battle line, I am sure the spirit of your soldiers will be lifted at the sight of their king returning," Michael told David.

"Why did the army not just come to the city and use the fortifications of Jerusalem to help them defeat the Edomites?" David asked Michael.

"Your people have been badly defeated and are greatly outnumbered. You have lost one-third of your army. They have been retreating, trying to make it back to the city. However, the Edomites have caught them, and the final battle will take place at first light."

"I do not understand," King David said to Michael. "I consulted the prophet Nathan and asked if the Lord would honor this battle and bring a great victory to his people. I was instructed to go. Why did the Lord lead his people down the pathway toward destruction?"

"I do not know the answer to that question. But what I do know is you and your people are surrounded by a magnificent army of angels that are here to defend you. You cannot see the army, but we are here. I will be in the army as well, and we will fight the demonic forces as you are fighting the Edomites. You are outnumbered, and victory will be difficult, but your job, King David, and our job, is to fight and to give every ounce of effort. Many will die, some will live, but we must remember, the battle is not ours, the battle is the Lord's.

Put your trust in the Lord. One more thing I have to share with you, David," Michael added. "Your son, Daniel, will accompany you to the battle and will defend you. He is a mighty warrior and a mighty defender."

With those words, the archangel Michael and Uri disappeared into the sky, riding their powerful horses to be with the army of angels.

David was stunned to hear the words from Michael that Daniel would accompany him to the battle line. Where was he? How would he get here? Would David really be fighting side by side with his son? As he was preparing to leave, David turned to Rafaella. "I do not wish for you to go with me into battle. I know you are a mighty warrior and a far greater fighter than I will ever be, but this is not your battle. Please remain here within the walls of Jerusalem and wait for our return."

"I traveled with you, David, so that I could see my brother, Rapha. Will Rapha be in the battle?" Rafaella knew the answer but asked the question anyway.

David answered truthfully, "Yes, I think he will be fighting with the Edomites against the Lord's people. He will come for me. I do not think he will rest until I am dead. He is fierce and evil, Rafaella, I do not think you will like what you see."

"I must see my twin. I must look into his eyes, and he must look into my eyes. I heard Michael say this is the Lord's battle, and I serve the Lord. I will fight with you, King David. Your soldiers will see my might and will see the power of a giant fighting for the cause of the Lord."

In truth, David was thankful Rafaella would be with his army. They could certainly use all the help they could get. They would be facing a strong, determined Edomite army that could taste victory.

The chariots of war would again be descending upon them, and of course, they would again be facing Rapha and his son, Lahmi.

David and Rafaella climbed onto the heavenly horse Michael had provided and together rode toward the battle line. The sight of blood and smell of death would soon dominate the landscape.

Michael was organizing the army of angels when Daniel and Hagan arrived. Angels are normally emotionless beings, their entire existence being to serve the purposes of the Lord and complete the tasks assigned to them. On occasion, though, angels can demonstrate emotion, usually in the form of shouting, singing, or even the raising and banging of swords. When the army of angels saw Hagan in his full angelic glory, harking back to his existence as the Defender of Defenders, a shout began that grew louder and louder until the entire spiritual realm could hear the shouts and hear the swords banging together. Hagan had returned.

Even archangel Michael let out a shout and held his sword, Tyrfing, up to the skies. It was said about Michael that he knew everything about everything and could never be surprised. But the return of Hagan definitely caught him by surprise and, for the first time Hagan could ever remember, the archangel was speechless. He just stared at the mighty angel.

Hagan broke the awkward stare down by saying, "Greetings, Michael, we are here to fight for the Lord." With the entire army of angels watching, Michael took his right hand and placed it behind the neck of Hagan, pulling the angel into him for an embrace between the two mightiest of warriors. He then took the left hand of Hagan and raised it to the sky. An Enochian chant of Jehovah-Jireh, the Lord will provide, broke out. All throughout the spiritual world, Jehovah-Jireh, Jehovah-Jireh, Jehovah-Jireh!

Daniel had Avigdor raised and was singing along with the angels as loudly as he could. Suddenly, Michael, Hagan, and Daniel were raised up to the heavens, disappearing from the army of angels. The three were caught up in a whirlwind and found themselves in heaven standing on top of the mountain of God. They heard the voice of God himself, "Who shall ascend the hill of the Lord? And who shall stand in his holy presence? He who has clean hands and a pure heart, who does not lift his soul to what is false, who walks blamelessly and does what is right. He who is willing to fight for the Lord and, also, willing to die for the Lord. I am the first, and I am the last."

Michael, Hagan, and Daniel all bowed before the voice. "Raise your eyes and let them gaze upon my son." All eyes lifted to see the sight of a man with a holy light abounding from him. He had a robe with a golden sash, white hair, eyes like blazing fire, feet like bronze. He held seven stars in his right hand, and a double-edged sword was coming out of his mouth. This is my beloved son, Jesus, the Savior of the world. He will be born into the world, and through his death and resurrection, humans will be offered forgiveness, salvation, and eternal life. His lineage will come from King David, and he will be a descendant of the son born to David and Bathsheba."

Jesus disappeared, but the voice of God continued, "King David must survive, and Bathsheba must be protected. Michael, you will relieve Mahlon and be charged with the protection of Bathsheba. Hagan, you will lead the army of my angels into battle against Lucifer and the demons. Daniel, you are now a mighty defender, and you will defend your father against the forces of evil. Stand." The three stood up with heads down, still facing the voice of God. "Daniel, you have been taught well by Hagan. You will defend righteousness in both the spiritual realm and the natural realm. Raise your head and receive the power that comes from the wings of the Lord that are now a part of you. You have flown before, but now you will fly under the strength of wings. Born to man, trained by angels, you are my defender." Daniel's body was transformed into one with powerful white wings, almost as large as Hagan's, protruding out of his shoulders and pointed toward the sky.

"Go and fight," said the voice of God.

Michael, Hagan, and Daniel were again amidst the army of angels, who were still chanting and singing praises to the Lord. When they saw Daniel and his wings, they sang even louder. So loud, in fact, that Lucifer and the hordes of demons took notice. Lucifer was incensed. His wrath and fury were disposed upon the demons who were worked up into a frenzy. Michael left to relieve Mahlon. Hagan took his place at the head of the army of angels. Daniel flew to stand beside his father in battle.

The demons attacked. Asmodeus led the demons as they slammed into the angelic forces. It would be impossible to estimate the number of demons; they seemed as numerous as the sand on a seashore and just kept coming and coming. The only way to kill a demon was to sever the head from its body with an angelic blade. The opposite was also true, as the only way to kill an angel was to take the head with a demonic blade. Heads were being taken from spiritual bodies as the two forces crushed into each other.

Asmodeus went directly for Hagan. He was surprised to see the mighty defender back in his original form. Lucifer had given him the assignment of defeating the army of angels, and he had assumed he would be fighting against the mighty archangel, Michael. "You look different from little Hadrach," Asmodeus said to Hagan as he drew his two swords, Death and Hell. "But you will suffer the same fate. You have been defeated once and will be again, only this time, you will not be cast into the Abyss, you will be dead forever. I will present your head as a trophy to Lord Lucifer."

Hagan pulled the Breather of Life from its scabbard and could feel the hunger and thirst for battle in its hilt. It had been a long time since Hagan had fought for the Lord. He must control his spirit and balance his body and mind. Hagan knew he was better than Asmodeus; he was more powerful and more skillful and more agile, yet he knew he was facing an extremely dangerous demon. Asmodeus was a killer and was very experienced in battle. He had fought and killed many angels, and he had fought and survived against archangel Michael. One slip or one error or a simple loss of focus would allow Death or Hell to be slicing through his neck. Hagan spoke to Asmodeus, "I would not want to be you facing me, the Defender of Defenders. This will not end well for you." Death followed by Hell attacked, each striking the mighty Breather of Life.

Lucifer had reappeared to Baal-Achbor, telling him to ready his army to withstand the advance of the Israelites. Rapha and Lahmi stood just outside the Edomite king's tent. "Their king has returned and will lead the attack just before dawn," Lucifer spoke to Baal-Achbor. "My giants will fight in the center of your army. You will position your chariots of war in front of the giants. As soon as the chariots spot the Israelites, they will charge, followed by my giants and your forces. My giants will be instructed to kill the king and any that try to protect him. I will be in the battle as well. You will fight to the end, there will be no retreat and no surrender. You will win, Baal-Achbor, or you will die. King David must not survive the battle. Should he live, you will not survive. You will either be killed by him or by me."

As the Edomite army prepared, Lucifer stood in front of his giants. He spoke first to Rapha, "You have failed me, Rapha. David lives and will lead the Israelites this very day." Out of nowhere, the red stick of Satan pounded into the temple of Rapha. "You are weak! You will kill David this day or you will suffer death at my hands!"

Another blow, this one to the forehead, causing blood to begin to flow down the face of the evil giant. Lucifer turned toward Lahmi. "If your father fails, you must be ready. You will drink his blood and eat his heart and take his place as giant of giants."

Lucifer's head turned into the head of the dragon and came right up to the face of Rapha. The giant could feel the heat and smell the stench of the breath coming out of the dragon's nostrils. The dragon said, "Tell me you will not let me down."

Rapha looked into the eyes of the dragon. "I will not fail you again, Father." As Rapha spoke, blood began to trickle out of both his ears.

"Good." The dragon slowly backed away.

The Edomite army could hear the roar. The badly outnumbered Israelites were letting out a roar that could be heard clear across the battlefield. King David had returned! Riding upon the heavenly horse, the king arrived in the camp before sunrise as the soldiers were preparing for their charge. A woman giant was with him! "Gather the forces," David told Benaiah.

The sky was just beginning to lighten as the Israelites gathered on the battle line in front of their king. "Brothers, it is good to see you again. The situation may seem bleak, and I will not lie to you and tell you we are not badly outnumbered. The enemy is strong and powerful and hungry to destroy you and to destroy our city behind us. This is not the place nor the time we would have chosen to fight this army, but this is the time and the place God has chosen. It may seem we are surrounded by the enemy, but a greater force surrounds us. We are surrounded by a great army of angels that are even now doing battle with the evil we are confronted with. This battle is not ours but is the Lord's. He will fight for us today, and he will defend us this day. Yes, many of us will die. We are not guaranteed to live and survive this battle. If we die, let us die with honor in the name of

Lord!" Another huge roar from the army. The king continued, "This is Rafaella, she will fight by our side today. She is a mighty warrior and is the twin sister to the evil Rapha. May the God of Gods, the Ancient of Days, the Great I am be with us!"

David drew a sword that had been given him by Joab and lifted it to the sky. "Jehovah-Jireh!" The Israelites drew their swords, lifted them and repeated their king, "Jehovah-Jireh! Jehovah-Jireh! Jehovah-Jireh!" The army ran into the face of death, the mighty Edomite chariots of war.

Just as David was about to encounter the Edomite war horses, he heard a powerful sound of wings flapping. The wings were producing a forceful breeze that blew throughout the army, and the entire force of Israelites stopped in their tracks and looked to the sky. Daniel had arrived! The warrior-defender landed directly in front of David, drew the mighty Avigdor, and shouted in Enochian, "Frm Lgt YH'WH!" For the Lord! The chariots smashed into the Israelites. Horses were screaming, soldiers were yelling, and blood began to flow from both men and horses. Daniel was roaring as he deposited his mighty sword into the hearts of horses. The banging sound of swords on swords escalated throughout the air. The Edomites kept coming, slowly driving their enemy backward. The only section of the Israelites that were not in retreat was King David, fighting alongside Daniel and Rafaella as they began to push forward, driving a wedge into the Edomites. No chariot could survive the onslaught of Daniel and Rafaella as they surrounded the king, protecting him from the deadly spears being thrown. Avigdor was killing chariot drivers, while Rafaella was using her speed and power to overcome the war horses. The last chariot was destroyed and fell to the ground, as Avigdor hungrily drove into the bone and tissues of the Edomite riders. Blood, organs, and other bodily fluids were flowing into the ground beneath them. Horse's eyes were wide as they breathed their last breath. Finally, their path was cleared, and Daniel, David, and Rafaella stepped forward into the presence of Rapha and Lahmi.

Lucifer, hovering behind the giants, concentrated his gaze on Rafaella. This was a surprise! He did not know about the female giant. How had this been kept from him? He was the prince of the earth. Surprise turned into anger as he realized he had been deceived all this time by Michael and the army of angels. No matter, they would pay the ultimate price for their deception.

The Edomites quickly fell in behind the trio of warriors as the rest of the Israelites continued to be driven backward. Daniel, King David, and Rafaella were surrounded and separated from the rest of their army.

Rapha's eyes were blinking, and he was trying to clear his head. He thought he was seeing some form of vision as he looked upon this female giant who was the exact same size as he. It was as if he was looking at the female version of himself. Rapha froze. Who was this? Lahmi too did not know what to say or do as he gazed upon this fellow giant.

Only Daniel could see Lucifer. He looked at Satan and felt fear. Evil seeped from his presence, and Daniel was unable to continue to look into his eyes. Daniel took a step backward as Lucifer told him, "It is right that you feel fear, young angel. Nothing can stand before me, and nothing can defeat me. I am the Morning Star and the Prince of Darkness, and I am the true God." David and Rafaella also felt the dark evil surrounding them. It was as if the air they were breathing was evil itself.

Daniel was fighting the fear. He thought of Hagan and what he had told him about confronting demons. He knew Lucifer could not harm him if he did not provoke him. Lucifer could not attack any of the three; he was forbidden by the Lord. Daniel's fight was with the giants Rapha and Lahmi.

Lucifer told Daniel, "I will give you one opportunity to join me and live. I will make you my chief demon, with authority that knows no bounds. You will be worshipped and obeyed, and your desires and dreams will be fulfilled. You will become more powerful than you could ever imagine. I know you want to slay these giants. I will let you kill them. In fact, you will replace them. You will be my son, and I will be your father. Join me!"

As Daniel listened to Lucifer, Rapha could not stop staring at Rafaella, who knew she must hurry if she hoped to change the heart of Rapha. "I am your sister, Rapha, your twin sister. Our mother's name is Sedena, and our father is the warrior angel called Hagan. That is right, your father is an angel of the Lord. You have angel blood flowing through your veins. Good blood. Holy blood. Your mother is still alive and is a strong believer in God. She worships the one true God. I worship and love the Lord as well. I know you have done many bad things, brother, but I am here to tell you, God can forgive you and rebuild you and use you for His glory. I have traveled this way not to fight you but so that you could look into my eyes and know that you are loved and that you do not have to be a slave to evil. I have come, Rapha, to take you home, to take you to your mother."

Daniel gathered up all the courage he could muster, looked into the eyes of Satan, and spoke, "I have a father, and he is right here next to me, and his army is going to be victorious this day. He will father a son, and through the lineage of that son, the Savior of the world will be born, to save all of mankind from sin, that whosoever believeth in him shall not perish but have eternal life."

Lucifer became the Red Dragon! He swung his giant tale at the back of the head of Rapha, knocking the giant off balance. "Kill this angel wannabe! Drive your sword through his heart!" Rapha drew two swords, one of them was David's blade, the sword of Goliath. Rapha attacked Daniel.

Lahmi moved forward to attack Rafaella, who stood in front of King David. "I do not want to fight you. You are my nephew, my flesh and blood." Lahmi, full of evil hatred, did not care; he would kill Rafaella with no remorse. She was nothing to him.

"Do not do this, Lahmi. I will not fight my brother, but I will kill you if I must," Rafaella took the blow from the sword of Lahmi, and her instincts for fighting and survival kicked in.

Lucifer watched. He was close to achieving his long-sought victory, the death of the prophecy, the death of David. There would be no coming Savior. He knew he only needed one of his giants to be successful. Whichever giant, Rapha or Lahmi, won their battle first would be rewarded with the honor of killing the king of Israel; there was no escape. As the Red Dragon watched, he knew he had one more move to make. Calling three demons to him, he gave them specific instructions and told them to hurry.

Daniel and Rapha went right at each other, each attempting to achieve a quick kill. Rapha was extradangerous as he yielded two swords, each capable of severing the head of Daniel. Avigdor was alive and beginning to get a feel of Rapha's swords and how he liked to use them. "Learn your enemy, understand your enemy, feel your enemy." Daniel could hear the words of Hagan in his mind as he used his great wings to move about Rapha, causing the big giant to slowly become frustrated. No one had ever really been able to offer Rapha a true challenge until this moment. Daniel was powerful and dangerous, and Rapha knew this would be a true fight to the death. The wings. The wings were disorienting Rapha. Every time he felt he could gain an advantage over Daniel, the wings would lift the warrior-defender and reposition him. Rapha realized he needed to drop a sword and try to use his powerful off hand to deliver blows.

As Rafaella and Lahmi fought, it was quickly apparent that Rafaella was the far superior fighter. Her speed and quickness were causing problems for Lahmi, who began to yell insults and spit into the face of Rafaella. Lahmi was trying to distract her so that she would make a mistake and leave her guard down, thereby allowing him to drive his sword into her heart.

King David watched as both fights were taking place. He tried to position himself to be able to help either Daniel or Rafaella but realized he was really confined by the Edomite army that had him surrounded. Daniel knew his father and knew he wanted to help, and so he yelled to him to stay out of the fight. "Stay safe! Let us defend you! Do not do anything foolish!" King David decided to honor the request of his son.

The fighting joy had come upon Daniel. He felt peace in his spirit. Knowing he had been chosen by the Lord to be taken to the Valley of Eternity, had been trained by Hagan, had been given this magnificent sword, Avigdor, blessed with wings from the Lord, he was fulfilling his purpose. His purpose was to kill Rapha and defend his father. He knew, and Rapha was beginning to realize, that he was too powerful for the giant. Rapha had dropped one of his swords, and each time Daniel attacked, he swung at the defender with his off hand. The blows would have normally devastated an opponent, but Daniel shrugged them off, seemingly becoming stronger. "You cannot hurt me. I fight in the name of our Lord!" Daniel said to Rapha. "You murdered my mother!" Daniel hit Rapha across the face with a monstrous blow. "I have been trained by your father, Hagan!" Another blow to the face of Rapha. "You are finished!"

Rapha was staggered and dropped his other sword. Blood was pouring from his face. His eyes were blurry, and blood again poured out of his ears. Drool was pouring from his mouth. Blood and sweat covered his body. He was about to pay for his life of evil. The hatred. The murders. The rapes. The destruction. The end had come for Rapha.

Rafaella had knocked Lahmi to the ground. He was no match for the twin of Rapha. She had pierced both shoulders with her blade, blood pouring out of his wounds. Lahmi was frothing at the mouth, and his eyes were wide with rage. Rafaella kicked his sword to the side, put her foot on his chest, and her blade was pressed into his neck. She was ready for the kill.

Lucifer was desperate. His giants were defeated. It was time for his last play.

CHAPTER 19

A horn in the distance. The royal horn of Edom. Three riders leading a fourth horse with a much smaller figure sitting atop. One of the three riders was King Baal-Achbor, who rode slightly out front of the others. The horn continued to blow, capturing the attention of Daniel, Rafaella, and David. Rapha was down to one knee and seemed to not even notice the sound of the horn, while Lahmi, swordless, still lay defeated under the foot and blade of Rafaella.

As Baal-Achbor and his two warriors led the fourth horse nearer to the battle line, Rafaella knew who the rider was. She recognized her mother, Sedena, stoically sitting atop the horse, hands tied behind her back. Rafaella could tell she was tired and hurt with bruises on her face. Her hair was disheveled, and her shoulders were slightly slumped. But she was doing her best to sit proud and wanted to appear unbroken.

Gadir's sons had safely delivered her to the port of Haifa whereby three men were introduced to her as friends who would help navigate her to Jerusalem. Nubia promised her these men could be trusted; little did he know the demons had entered their minds and their hearts and were following the orders of Lucifer. The men soon beat her, tied her, and led her to the king of the Edomites, Baal-Achbor.

As Daniel was about to drive Avigdor into the heart of Rapha, Rafaella yelled for him to "Hold!" She spoke to Daniel from the deepest part of her heart. "Please allow my brother to see his mother before he dies. Let his eyes gaze upon the godly woman who bore him many years ago."

Daniel wanted to end the life of the evil giant. It was his purpose. Yet, he could also feel the passion in the voice of Rafaella. He looked at Sedena, remembering the story of Hadrach and their love. In honor of Hagan and out of respect to Sedena, he made his decision. He ordered Rapha to stand, turn around and see his mother.

Baal-Achbor took the reins of the horse and led Sedena within several feet of Rapha. Sedena looked into the eyes of her son. Her tears flowed. She could not help herself. What she saw was not her son, not the baby that had been stolen from her. She saw evil, filth, and nastiness. Was her son in there anywhere? Was there any flame still flickering within his soul? She spoke. "Where are you, Rapha? I am your mother, and I want you to know something. You have been lied to all these years. You were not born to be evil. You were not born to worship Lucifer. And he is not your father. Your father was the greatest of all angelic defenders. He loved you. You were born out of love. I want you to know I love you! I love you, Rapha! And God loves you!"

Rapha's eyes stared and began to clear slightly. He could not speak and knew he was about to meet his death. He deserved to die. Deep in his heart, as his mother told him that she loved him, Rapha felt something he had never felt before. He was not sure what it was, but it was different. It did not come from Lucifer, and it did not come from Namok, and it was not demonic. It was almost as if icy water had been thrown onto a fire, and he was simmering inside. The hate inside him had been extinguished.

Daniel could see Lucifer. No longer the Red Dragon, he was approaching King Baal-Achbor. He stood behind him, almost becoming one with him. As Daniel was about to act, he heard a voice in his ears. It was clear and was specific and carried authority. It was the voice of Michael, the archangel. "Get David out now! Bring him to me!" There was no ambiguity and no debating. This was a direct order. Daniel turned immediately, grabbed his father, and let his powerful wings carry him skyward. Hordes of demons, screeching and hissing, followed and chased. Daniel let his wings carry them as it seemed they knew exactly where to go.

Daniel approached Michael, standing at the entrance of Adoni's cave. Tyrfing was drawn, and the archangel was glowing in brightness and power. As the demons saw Michael, they stopped, hesitant to attack the angel of angels. One demon dared, flying straight at the heart of Michael. Tyrfing made quick work at severing the head. No other demon wanted any part of the archangel as they backed away, eventually leaving altogether.

Daniel set David down in front of Michael. "Well done, Daniel, thank you," said Michael. "You have done well so far. You will return to battle. Hagan will need your help."

Daniel looked at his father and they embraced. "I love you, son. Go and fulfill your purpose."

Lucifer was whispering into the mind of Baal-Achbor. He felt rage as he saw Daniel leaving with David. His plan to slay the king of the Israelites and destroy the prophecy of the Lord was finished for now. Vengeance and destruction all he had remaining. He would make them suffer. Daniel would suffer, Rapha would suffer, this woman, Sedena, would suffer, the female giant would suffer. And, of course, Hagan would suffer. Lucifer knew he was not permitted to harm Sedena, but he could command the king of the Edomites to do as he wished. He wrapped his fingers around his head and squeezed ever so tightly. "I want the woman dead. You will slash her throat in front of her son and daughter."

Baal-Achbor grabbed the woman and dragged her off the horse. Rapha froze. Rafaella screamed as she took her foot off Lahmi and turned to attack the king of Edomites. The blade was at Sedena's throat, the voice of Lucifer could be heard. "Rapha, you have failed me. Now watch as your mother's life is taken from her!"

The blade slid into the back of Rafaella, coming out the front of her chest. Lahmi had risen, grabbed his sword, and plunged it into the back of Rafaella. She stumbled in front of Rapha, falling to her knees, staring up into the eyes of her brother. Sedena was hysterical, crying, sobbing, "No! No! No! My daughter!"

Rafaella was dying. She looked again into the face of her brother and muttered the last words she would ever speak, "Do not let me die in vain. Fight for me, brother." She fell on her side, and her eyes looked up to the sky. The last sight her eyes would see upon this earth was her father, the mighty Hagan, flying directly at King Baal-Achbor. He was beautiful, powerful, full of light, hair flowing, enormous wings moving with the wind, his sword, the Breather of Life, in his right hand, the head of Asmodeus in his left. He plunged the Breather of Life into the heart of Baal-Achbor. Rafaella was gone. Her spirit rising into the arms of angels waiting to carry her toward her heavenly home.

The Defender of Defenders had arrived. Baal-Achbor was dead. Sedena had fainted when she saw Hagan, and Rapha turned to face his son, Lahmi.

Rapha picked up the sword of Goliath, David's sword, and with his left hand, he delivered a crushing blow across the temple of Lahmi. Lucifer shouted at Lahmi, "Kill him! Kill your father!" Rapha hit him again. Staggering, Lahmi tried to retrieve his blade from the body of Rafaella, but as he pulled, he was hit again, this time falling to his knees. Pulling the blade free, he barely had time to block the sword of Goliath as Rapha attacked mercilessly. Blow after blow was delivered. Lahmi, finally stumbling to his feet, retreated. "There is no escape," Rapha told his son. Full of fury, Rapha swung, knocking the blade from the hands of Lahmi.

Rapha dropped his sword and began punching Lahmi with his bare hands. Unable to block the blows, Lahmi succumbed to the vicious fists pounding into his face. Teeth broken, blood spurting from his nose and eyes swollen shut, Lahmi knew he was finished. Rapha finally took his right hand and placed it around the throat of his son. Using his enormous strength, he turned Lahmi so that he could look into the eyes of Lucifer as he squeezed the life from the giant. Rapha felt a release as he squeezed. The evil in him was being released, pouring out of his spirit, emptying from his body. It was as if he was purging himself from all the wicked deeds he had performed. As the last breaths of life were coming from Lahmi, Rapha shouted at Lucifer, "You are not my father, and I do not belong to you anymore!" One last squeeze, the throat was crushed, and blood was flowing from the carotid artery. One final gasp for air, and Lahmi was gone. Rapha felt the blood from his son spurting into his face. He let it come, refusing to divert it as it poured into his eyes and mouth. Rapha let out a primal scream that could be heard throughout both the physical and the spiritual world.

The scream from Rapha was suddenly silenced as the tail from the Red Dragon wrapped itself around his neck. "You are nothing but a worthless piece of shit," the dragon said as the tail dragged Rapha to the ground.

Hagan slammed into the dragon. "I have brought you the head of Asmodeus," Hagan spoke to Lucifer the dragon. He tossed the head at the dragon's feet as he swung the mighty Breather of Life into the tail, severing it from the dragon's body and saving the life of Rapha, who lay motionless upon the ground.

Lucifer let out a scream and reverted to his original form. He drew Abaddon and spoke in Enochian. "There will be no mercy this time, Hagan. You will not be cast into the Abyss. I will take your life from you. You are about to discover the true power of the Prince of Darkness, the Morning Star. There is no one to save you now!"

Sedena had regained consciousness, and sitting up, she looked and could see Hagan as he faced the most evil sight she had ever seen. She saw true evil, flaming and furious, obscene bright redness coming from his presence. He looked horrific, a monstrous madness displayed completely in his malicious face. Lucifer was a beautiful savage, ready to rip apart anything that stood in his way. His blade, the bloodthirsty Abaddon, caught fire. Horns began to emerge from his forehead, and a strange star became visible on his chest. There were symbols in the star. A black smoke came from both his nostrils and ears. He smelled of death. In his left hand, he held a ball of fire.

Sedena felt a fear she had never felt before. It was not a fear for herself. It was fear for Hagan.

Lucifer threw the ball of fire into the face of Hagan. He was temporarily blinded as Lucifer hit him full force with horns from his forehead. Hagan was knocked backward through the air as Lucifer held Abaddon high above his head. Abaddon drove for the kill but was blocked in the last second by the blade of Avigdor.

Daniel had arrived! Daniel had entered the battle, giving up his immunity to an attack from Lucifer. He would fight side by side with Hagan against the Morning Star. A smile came across the face of Lucifer as he said, "Welcome to hell, boy."

The power of Lucifer was a power Daniel had never felt before. As mighty as Daniel had become and as splendid a sword as Avigdor was, the blows delivered to Lucifer seemed to have no effect whatsoever. "Control your spirit!" yelled Hagan as the two surrounded Lucifer, each focusing on the sword, Abaddon. They flew through the sky, disappearing from the view of Sedena, who was praying to the Lord to protect both Hagan and Daniel.

Lucifer was using both Abaddon and his red stick to defend the blows from Avigdor and Breather of Life. He had not unleashed his full fury yet, had not gone on the attack but seemed to be leading Hagan and Daniel as they fought throughout the spiritual realm. Hagan realized they were being led, but the battle joy had come upon him, and he was fully committed to seeing this through to the end. He was also worried for Daniel, although the young defender seemed to be holding his own so far. Suddenly, a red fog engulfed them, and Hagan knew immediately where they were. They had arrived at the gates of Namok. "Welcome to the true kingdom, Daniel," Lucifer spoke.

Then Satan attacked.

Abaddon was a blazing fury, being swung in all directions, knocking both Hagan and Daniel off balance. A new red dragon's tail emerged from Lucifer's backside, with razor sharp spikes, and it drew blood as it raked across the cheek of Daniel. "You will bow to me, boy! You will serve me! I will be your Lord!" Lucifer was shouting at Daniel.

Hagan was spinning to his left in the air, and as he landed, he switched Breather of Life into his left hand and surprised Lucifer with a thrust, penetrating the devil's skin just above the heart. He followed with a smashing blow from his right hand that landed squarely across the horns. Hagan was in his full glory, fighting in his original strength and power. His entire presence blossomed with a whiteness that seemed to grow brighter as the battle continued. He now knew Lucifer did not intend to kill Daniel but was going to recruit him into his legions, into Namok, and was going to forcibly make him bow and worship and obey him. Hagan knew he could not let that happen. He spread his wings, lifting himself above Lucifer, then dove at him from above, Breather of Life pointed at the skull of Satan.

As Hagan went to deliver his blade into the head of Lucifer, Daniel was thrusting Avigdor at his heart. They were going to take the brain and the heart of Satan. Both blades, however, Breather of Life and Avigdor, suddenly smashed into an impenetrable shield that enveloped around Lucifer. The shield of Satan. The shield was not visible and had seemingly come out of nowhere. Hagan had never seen Lucifer fully protected by this shield, but he could remember hearing the legend that Lucifer was only permitted to use the safeguard within the vicinity of Namok. Lucifer laughed as Hagan and Daniel each delivered blows that continually had no effect on him, bouncing off the invisible armament that protected him.

The gates of Namok opened.

"Come, Daniel, come into my kingdom, and I will give you the world." Daniel swung again. "You cannot defeat me," Lucifer calmly told him.

Daniel attempted another lunge but was caught midair by the long right hand of Satan reaching through the shield. The hand of Satan grasped the throat of Daniel. "You are now mine, you belong to me. Welcome to your new home, my son." Lucifer stepped toward the gates, carrying Daniel with him.

Hagan was screaming and delivering blow after blow into the shield, the safeguard protecting the Prince of Darkness. Each blow continued to be deflected. As Lucifer and Daniel were taking their last steps into the gates of Namok, Hagan pointed his wings to the sky, lifted the Breather of Life heavenward, and shouted, "My Lord, my Lord, for your kingdom, for your defender, for Daniel, I ask for the strength to break this shield! Save Daniel, my God! Save Daniel!"

Hagan brought down the Breather of Life with all the might he could muster. The blade crashed into the shield of Satan. As the blade crashed, the shield shattered. The mighty Breather of Life, sword of Hagan, also shattered into hundreds of pieces.

Stunned from the blow, Lucifer turned to face Hagan. He momentarily loosened his grip from the throat of Daniel, allowing Daniel to wrestle free and retreat behind Hagan.

"Fly, Daniel. Leave this place," Hagan said. He turned and looked at Daniel in the eyes. "You must deliver a message for me. Tell Sedena how much I loved her."

Daniel's eyes were filling with tears. "Come with me, Hagan, let us fly together!"

"No, young Daniel. That is not my purpose. You must go now!"

"Take my sword. Take Avigdor," Daniel said as he offered Hagan his blade.

"No, that is your sword given to you by the Lord, and you will continue to use it for His mighty purposes. Go now!"

Hagan then spoke his last words to Daniel. "I love you."

Daniel flew with tears streaming down his face.

Lucifer drove the flaming Abaddon into the gut of Hagan. Then dragging the mighty defender by the hair, Lucifer and Hagan disappeared into Namok as the gates shut behind them.

CHAPTER 20

Daniel returned to find the army of Israelites, gaining the advantage against the Edomites. His spirit was a combination of sadness and anger. He needed a good fight and decided to join the Israelites as they drove the Edomites back southward toward their homeland.

Entering the tent of Joab, Daniel found the army commander reviewing the battle plans to be executed next morning. Joab immediately stopped his planning, stood, and said, "Hello, Daniel. It is good to see you again. You are always welcome within this army. Do you bring news?"

"The only news I bring is the news that I am ready to join you in the battle against the Edomites. How is the battle progressing?" Joab responded, "Very well, the enemy has become very discouraged and seems to have lost the heart for battle. Many of their soldiers have deserted and fled home. The death of their king, Baal-Achbor, greatly diminished the spirit of their army. I feel as if one or two more aggressive strikes into their weakened fortifications will end the confrontation."

"Very well," said Daniel. "I will join you in the attack tomorrow." As Daniel prepared to leave, he turned and asked Joab, "Where will I find the giant, Rapha?"

"He has been chained and imprisoned. We will bring him back with us to Jerusalem to stand trial for the monstrosities he is accused of."

"I would like to see him," Daniel said.

Daniel was led to the barracks where Rapha was chained hand and foot. He entered, telling the guard he wished to speak to the giant alone. Rapha sat upon a wooden box with head facing the ground. He was clearly disheartened, showing no signs of his former self. *Hopeless* is the word that came to Daniel's mind as he saw the giant. "He has lost the will to live. He has lost all hope. Totally alone. Totally abandoned," thought Daniel. "Look at me," Daniel spoke to Rapha.

Rapha's eyes slowly lifted as he looked upon the defender. His eyes were different, no longer filled with the evil hatred but, instead, reflected defeat and sadness. "And so we meet again?" asked Daniel.

"Yes," Rapha quietly responded.

"Do you know my purpose and my mission for which I have been trained?" Rapha shook his head. Daniel continued, "I have been trained by the angels in heaven. I have lived in the Valley of Eternity and have been raised by the great defenders. God has commissioned me to be a great defender for His people. He has given me my sword and my wings and has prepared me for my great purpose."

Rapha was listening. His head was up, and he was looking at Daniel as he continued speaking, "I want you to know what I have been trained for." Daniel drew Avigdor from its scabbard. Rapha's eyes widened as he gazed at the great blade up close. A light was coming from the blade as Daniel pointed it out toward the giant. "I have been trained to protect God's people, to protect the king of Israel, and I have been trained to kill. My purpose is to kill you, Rapha. I also want you to know who trained me. I have been trained by your father, the mighty Hagan, the defender of defenders. I loved your father, and I want you to know, Rapha, he loved you as well. He knew that the evil had overcome you, and he knew you had committed immense atrocities against mankind. He knew you must die, but, at the same time, he still loved you."

Rapha's eyes were filled with tears.

"Your father was a mighty warrior. But he also did many things during his lifetime that caused him regret. He too turned his back on the Lord. Hagan had been a follower of Lucifer and had been cast from heaven. God chose to forgive him and offered him a new life and a new spirit and a new calling. Stand up, Rapha," Daniel said. As the giant stood, Daniel took Avigdor and lifted the blade up toward the sky. "My purpose has been to kill you, Rapha, but the Lord has changed my purpose and has given me the honor to be the one who informs you the Lord has forgiven you." Daniel placed Avigdor upon the head of Rapha. "You are forgiven. You are loved. You are set free." With a sudden movement, Avigdor struck the chains upon the wrists and feet of Rapha. "You are now my brother," Daniel said.

Rapha was now fully crying. He fell to his knees and dropped his head to the ground. In between sobs, he was giving thanks. "Thank you, Lord, thank you, Lord, thank you, Lord."

Daniel and Rapha entered the tent of Joab. Daniel addressed the commander, "I want you to know, Joab, that tomorrow we will defeat the Edomites. Rapha has been set free by the Lord, and he will fight for the Lord's people."

Daniel and Rapha fought side by side against the Edomites, who could not withstand the onslaught and eventually fled back to their own land.

Rafaella's body was carried back to Haifa, the place of her birth. King David arranged and attended her funeral. Sedena stood next to her son, Rapha, as the body was lowered into the ground. Daniel, hovering in the air above the grave, played his harp. As he was playing, he realized he was not just playing for Rafaella. He was playing for his mother, Abigail, and he was playing for Hagan, the Defender of Defenders.

After the funeral, Sedena traveled with Rapha to Jerusalem. She would live out the remainder of her days in the city of her God. David provided her living quarters and assigned Lizona to be her handmaiden. Daniel delivered to Sedena the message he had been asked to deliver. He told her of Hagan and all that he had done for him. The guidance, the training, the mentorship, the love he had shown him. He told her, "You were the love of his life." Sedena looked at Daniel and told him, "I am sure Hagan found great joy in his purpose of training you. I was not the only one he loved. I know he loved you as well. I believe he would be proud for you to replace him as Defender of Defenders."

Rapha was offered and accepted an appointment as a member of King David's household guard. It would take time for the Israelites to be comfortable around and to trust the giant of giants, but the king made sure everyone knew he was forgiven. In time, the people would grow to love Rapha, son of Hagan.

David once again ruled the kingdom. Daniel and Lizona stood together and watched as all of Jerusalem gathered in the center of the city to celebrate the victory over the Edomites with praise and feasting and sacrifices to the Lord. They listened to the words of their king, David:

> *I will exalt you, my God the King; I will praise your*
>   *name for ever and ever.*
> *Every day I will praise you and extol your name for*
>   *ever and ever.*
> *Great is the Lord and most worthy of praise; his*
>   *greatness no one can fathom.*

Our generation will commend your works to
another; They will tell of your mighty acts.
They will speak of the glorious splendor of your maj-
esty, and I will meditate on your
Wonderful works.
They will tell of the power of your awesome works,
and I will proclaim your great deeds.
They will celebrate your abundant goodness and
joyfully sing of your righteousness.

All of Judah and all of Israel praised the Lord their God.

"Where will you go, and what will you do?" Lizona asked Daniel. In truth, Daniel was not sure. He had not received any message nor had any communication with any angel since the end of the battle. Lizona gently took Daniel's hands into hers, turning to face the defender. "Stay here in Jerusalem. Stay here with your father, and with your people. Stay here with me." Lizona pulled Daniel close to her, and they kissed. Daniel felt her warmth and the softness of her lips and the smell of her hair. He knew he could easily fall in love with this beautiful girl. Perhaps, he already had. As they were kissing, Daniel opened his eyes and, in the distance, he saw the horse. He saw Pran. The archangel riding atop with Uri and his mount close behind leading a third beautiful white stallion, which had no rider. The horses stopped in the distance and patiently waited.

Daniel gently stepped back from Lizona, still holding her hands. "Lizona, my purpose has not been fulfilled. I must leave, and I do not know when I will return. I do not know when I can see you again and can make no promises. I do not know the plans the Lord has for me."

Lizona's eyes welled with tears, but she was determined to be strong. "Daniel, I know you must leave. I know our God has mighty plans for you. But I also know you will return. I will wait for you, and I will pray for you every day." She kissed him one final time, then whispered in his ear, "I love you." She was gone, walking away into the crowd of people.

Daniel turned and flew to the archangel. "Greetings, Michael."

"Greetings, defender," Michael responded.

Daniel spoke, "I did not know if I would see you again after my failure. I feel like I let everyone down outside the gates of Namok."

"You let no one down, young Daniel," said Michael. "Your purpose was complete. David was safely protected, and the evil in Rapha was destroyed."

"But what about Hagan?" Daniel asked. "I feel like I failed him."

"Hagan too served his purpose. He knew he was to protect and defend you to the end, and that is what he did." Michael continued, "This battle has come to an end, Daniel, but the great war continues."

Daniel climbed onto the back of the beautiful white stallion. "The horse is yours," Michael told him.

"Can I name him?" asked Daniel.

"Yes, he is yours to name," responded the archangel.

"His name shall be Hadrach."

The bells were ringing as Ishboth opened the mighty gates into the Valley of Eternity. Michael entered, followed by Uri and Daniel. The angels were gathered in the sky. White was everywhere.

As he listened to the bells, Daniel's mind was marinating on the words of Michael, "The great war continues." He knew that he would soon fly again into battle.

AFTERWORD

David was the father of Solomon, whose mother
    was Bathsheba,
Solomon the father of Rehoboam,
Rehoboam the father of Abijah,
Abijah the father of Asa,
Asa, the father of Jehoshaphat,
Jehoshaphat the father of Jehoram,
Jehoram the father of Uzziah,
Uzziah the father of Jotham,
Jotham the father of Ahaz,
Ahaz the father of Hezekiah,
Hezekiah the father of Manasseh,
Manasseh the father of Amon,
Amon the father of Josiah,
And Josiah the father of Jeconiah and his broth-
    ers at the time of the exile to Babylon.
After the exile to Babylon:
Jeconiah was the father of Shealtiel,
Shealtiel the father of Zerubbabel,
Zerubbabel the father of Abiud,
Abiud the father of Eliakim,
Eliakim the father of Azor,
Azor the father of Zadok,
Zadok the father of Akim,

Akim the father of Eliud,
Eliud the father of Eleazar,
Eleazar the father of Matthan,
Matthan the father of Jacob,
And Jacob the father of Joseph, the husband of
     Mary, of whom was born Jesus, who is called
     Christ. (*Matthew 1:6–16*)

EPILOGUE

Daniel could not rest. The only thing on his mind was Hagan. He had let him down. The Valley of Eternity was not the same anymore. As he sat high atop the tree of Hagan, Daniel could still sense his presence, hear his voice, feel his spirit. Was Hagan even alive? What had happened to him within the fires of Namok?

The emptiness inside of him would not leave. One question repeatedly came into his mind: "What would Hagan do if the roles were reversed?" Daniel knew. Hagan would not rest.

How long he had been back in the valley, Daniel had no idea. His angel training had forced him to abandon his human concept of time. If he had to guess, Daniel would say he had been back for two or three weeks. Too long.

The valley was still. No sound could be heard. Even the water from the River of Hope was still. Daniel quietly flew out of the tree and sailed through the air to the gate on the southern end. Waiting patiently for as long as he could stand, Daniel finally pounded his fist upon the middle bar of the gate. Nothing. Again, he pounded, this time with more force. Suddenly, Ishboth appeared out of the bars of the gate. "Yes, what is it, Daniel? What do you need?"

"I need to leave the valley. Please open the gate for me."

"I have no notification for your exit from the valley. No instructions. I cannot open the gate without instructions. It is forbidden," replied Ishboth.

"There is a matter that I must take care of, Ishboth. I will return as quickly as possible."

"I am sorry, Daniel. Perhaps we should call Michael and ask for his permission. The gate will not open without specific instructions and permission. Again, it is forbidden."

Daniel's hand reached toward his scabbard, and he drew Avigdor. He did not want to threaten Ishboth, who he knew was simply performing his purpose as gatekeeper, but he knew the time was short, and he needed to leave immediately.

"Ishboth, I am sorry it has to be this way, but I want you to know that I am leaving the valley with or without your help. We can do this the easy way, or we can do it the hard way. It is your choice."

Daniel took a step toward Ishboth, who froze in bewilderment.

"Please do not do this, Daniel. Let us talk to Michael. I am sure he will be willing to hear you out. I will not open the gate for you at this time." Ishboth went to one knee, willing to sacrifice his life before he opened the gate without permission. Daniel stared at him. He was not thinking clearly. He needed to see Hagan, hear his voice, undo the wrong he felt he had done him. Placing the tip of Avigdor at the throat of Ishboth, Lucifer's voice was suddenly in his ears. He heard Lucifer speak, "Do it! Come to me! I will free Hagan for you!" Daniel raised his sword for the death blow.

As Daniel began to swing, a noose wrapped around his chest, and he was violently thrust backward, falling upon his back as he lost the grip of Avigdor. He struggled to get the noose off his chest, heaving and gasping for breath as it gripped his chest tighter and tighter. Turning his head around, Daniel gazed into the fury of the archangel, Michael.

Michael's body was totally engulfed in light, his eyes were fire, anger all upon his face, his authority and power on full display. Holding his left hand out, Avigdor obediently flew into his palm.

His voice was thunder as it proclaimed, "You have a choice to make, Daniel, defender of defenders. You will yield, or you will die at the hands of your own sword, Avigdor!"

Daniel immediately knew he was in the wrong, had allowed emotion to overtake him. In his quest to leave the valley in order to avenge Hagan, he had acted outside his purpose, and in his quest to avenge Hagan, he had allowed the voice of Lucifer to enter into his mind. "I yield, Michael! I am sorry," he said as the tears of regret began to form in his eyes.

Michael loosened the noose before drawing it off Daniel and back into his right hand. "You do not have permission to leave the valley at this time. Your next purpose has yet to be revealed by our Lord. You must let go of your emotion and let go of your guilt and submit to whatever purpose the Lord will present for you. A defender must never act outside the will of God."

Daniel stood up and turned to Ishboth. "I am sorry for my actions. I was wrong. Please accept my apology."

Ishboth stepped toward Daniel and placed his hand upon his cheek. "Daniel, we all hurt for Hagan, and I understand your pain, but we must allow the Lord to guide all of our actions. I do accept your apology and will never speak of this confrontation again."

"Thank you, Ishboth."

Michael felt the spirit of the Lord filling his mind.

"Our God is speaking to me even now at this moment, young Daniel." He released Avigdor back into the hand of Daniel. "He will allow you to leave the valley and travel to the Gates of Namok. You will stand before the gates. But you will not stand alone. I will stand beside you! I do not know what our actions or purpose will be once we arrive at Namok. We will trust in the Lord."

Daniel did not know what to say. The words would not come. Bowing his head to Michael, the only words he could get out were "Thank you, Michael."

Pran appeared, followed by Hadrach. Michael glided onto the back of his angelic stallion while Daniel replaced Avigdor into his scabbard before climbing upon the back of Hadrach, the angelic warhorse that had been given to him. Michael spoke, "You may open the gate, Ishboth."

As Michael and Daniel approached the Gates of Namok, Daniel was filled with the thought that they were far from home.

ABOUT THE AUTHOR

Brent Jackson is a high school history teacher and football coach. He lives in Cumming, Georgia, with his wife, Wendy, and six children. *Defender: A Story of Angels and Demons* is the first novel in the *Defender* series. He holds degrees from Georgia Southern University and Georgia State University. When he is not teaching, coaching, or writing, Brent spends his time running marathons and riding motorcycles.